TIMELESS

A story of devotion.

G.A.HAUSER

*allow your imagination to
wander...
suspend your reality
and your craving
for explanations
and reasons...
for love knows no
bounds,
and fiction can take you
anywhere you let it
bring you.
so let go of yourself,
make-believe
and know
there is only love
and that is all.*

TiMELESS

G. A. HAUSER

TiMELESS

CHAPTER 1

Dr Terry Lennox woke with a start.

As if he had been under water and needed air, he inhaled a gasp of breath and then gripped the bedding. He lay still, listening, trying to figure out where he was. It was dark and smelled of mold. Terry could see the wall in front of him was bare, a rectangle of light shined from between the curtains on the window, a streetlight, or the moon, Terry didn't know which. He sat up slowly and rubbed his face, unable to recall.

He made it to his feet and using the wall for balance he walked to an open door and entered a bathroom, turning on the light.

The brightness made him wince and squint.

Slowly he opened his eyes to get used to the glare and looked into the mirror over the sink vanity. He touched his scruffy jaw and stared at his reflection.

A man appearing to be in his late teens or early twenties, handsome, with blue eyes and jet black shaggy hair was looking back at him.

Terry inspected his features and then stared at his muscular chest and tight powerful frame. He splashed his face and leaned both hands on the sink, inspecting his square jaw line and the slight cleft in his chin. After a critique of his reflection, Terry looked around the small bathroom. An off-white shower curtain, moldy at the bottom, hung around the tub; a bar of soap and washcloth were on a shelf built into the white tile wall.

G. A. HAUSER

Terry left the bathroom and turned on the light. A single bed with a worn blanket and pillow, dressed in graying sheets, was against the wall under the window. One standing lamp was beside it, along with a duffle bag and a pile of clothing near army-style boots. Terry walked to the window and peered out of the curtain.

The avenue under his window could be anywhere. Main Street, USA. The brick and windowpane façades of the retail stores were dark, closed for the night. Then Terry noticed a car drive by. He jumped startled at the make and model. Waiting to make sure what he was seeing wasn't someone's classic automobile, Terry spotted another, same year, different make.

"Nineteen sixty?" He leaned on the glass, looking down at the street for more clues.

Wanting to know where he was, Terry looked through the pile of clothing on the floor and stepped into a pair of pants, putting a tight white T-shirt over his head. He patted the pockets for a wallet, anything. Searching the contents of the room, Terry noticed a hotel key and picked it up. It had a plastic tab with his room number on it. He pocketed it and left the room, walking in his bare feet to the staircase and trotting down to the lobby.

The front desk was vacant; a bell was on the counter for service. Terry disregarded it and hunted around the lobby, finding what he was looking for. A newspaper.

He picked it up and read the front page.

The Bergen County Record, New Jersey, May 5, 1961.

He read the featured headline article.

Astronaut Alan B. Shepard Jr. became America's first space traveler as he made a fifteen-minute suborbital flight in a capsule launched from Cape Canaveral, Fla.

Terry dropped the newspaper on the table where he had found it and returned to his room. He turned the hotel key and closed the door behind him.

TiMELESS

This is the wrong year. I'm here too early. How did we get this wrong?

He placed the key on the dresser and sat on the worn out bed. Terry rubbed his face tiredly and stared into space. There was nothing he could do now. He had to deal with what he had until he moved on. If...he moved on.

He lay back down on the bed and tried to sleep until morning. Terry curled into a ball, closing his eyes, wondering how this project was going to succeed. Though he wanted it to be an easy task, he knew in his heart, this would most likely fail, and he would be lost, wandering in a past year, without hope.

Trying not to doubt the science from his own era, Terry nodded off, until the morning light filled the small room.

~

Opening his eyes, Terry heard voice coming through the thin walls; a man and woman talking over music. *Stand By Me* by Ben E. King was playing. Terry could hear it clearly over the discussion...or argument, the couple was having.

He sat up and rubbed his face, forcing himself to function. He had to. Something had brought him here to this day, this year, and although Terry did believe in random acts, his mathematics told him differently. There had to be a reason he was here.

He entered the bathroom, turning on the water in the shower and stripping off his briefs. As he washed he hoped his time here in 1961 wouldn't be long. No computers? No cell phones? Terry wasn't sure he was ready for that.

He washed quickly and stepped out of the tub, using a double edged razor he found in a small leather kit to shave his coarse jaw. He could see himself in his eyes in the reflection. But Terry imagined to the world around him, he was not Terry Lennox, he was the handsome young stud in the mirror.

Rinsing the foam off his face and neck, Terry returned to the bedroom and sorted, in the light of day, all the items in the room. He finally found a wallet and read the name on the driver's license. Shannon Albright, age nineteen. There was cash, but not much, and a Pontiac car key on a keychain with the car company logo. Terry packed all his clothing and dressed in a pair of beige slacks and a cotton shirt. He hoisted his duffle bag over his shoulder and left the hotel room, intent on finding his car and driving to the address on the ID. It was local, so Terry knew the man's body he occupied must have family here.

He left the hotel and began hunting for a Pontiac which opened when he turned the key in the lock.

The sun was warming the early May day, and pedestrians walked up and down the pavement, wearing everything from business attire to casual tops and flared skirts ala late fifties era style.

A red Pontiac Ventura opened when Terry pushed the key in the lock. Terry tossed his bag in the back seat and sat behind the wheel, starting it up. A muscle car. He smiled. *Good taste, Shannon. You're all macho man.* He opened the glove compartment and found a map. Unfolding it, Terry looked for the address that was on the ID. No satellite navigation, no internet routes. He either had to figure it out from the map, or stop and ask someone directions.

He located the street on the large awkward map and wasn't far from it. After folding the unwieldy paperwork, Terry pulled out of the parking space, cranking down the window with a handle. When he turned on the radio, *Dedicated to the One I Love* by the Shirelles came out of the mono-speaker.

Terry rested his arm on the open window and tried not to be distracted by the 1950's cars and trucks driving around him. It felt as if he were playing a role in a movie or part of a computer graphic.

He passed a service station seeing the price per gallon was thirty-one cents. He choked at the sight and shook his head. "Unreal." Not

TiMELESS

only that, a man in a uniform with a cap was washing the windshield of the car getting gas. A lost world.

Terry slowed down when he approached the street he was looking for. He drove through the neighborhood, seeing lawn sprinklers keeping the grass green, large maple and elm trees full of spring foliage, shady and peaceful, and a row of 1940's Cape Cod style houses, each with attached one-car garages and white cement driveways.

He parked in front of the address and sat staring at it. Terry left his duffle bag in the car, and didn't even bother to roll up the window. No car alarm, no key fob remote to arm it, and probably no crime.

Keeping his eye on the front door, Terry trotted up the stone path between two trimmed hedges and glanced at the flowering azaleas and hydrangeas that framed either side of the porch. There was a milk-box on the front stoop which completely amazed him. He looked down at his key ring and before he tried one key in the lock, he turned the knob. The door opened.

"Hello?" he called as he entered.

A pretty woman in her forties immediately appeared, wearing an apron over her dress and wiping her hands on a towel. "Shannon!"

"Mom?" Terry figured by her age and clothing; a flaring printed dress, her hair style appearing slightly stiff, as if sprayed with clear gloss, that this woman had to be his mother.

She raced to him and hugged him.

He hugged her back, wondering why he was in a hotel when his mother seemed to be happy to see him.

She sniffled and dabbed her eye at her emotion. "I'm so glad you came back. I told your father you'd come to your senses."

Terry inspected the living room. A big lumbering stereo console took up an entire wall and the furniture was dark blue fabric. A wood and plastic chandelier from a chain over a black faux leather chair and ottoman and a fake tree stood in the corner.

"Are you hungry? Let me make you breakfast." She held his hand and led him to the kitchen.

Terry suddenly knew the meaning of 50's kitsch. Formica and aluminum table and chairs, white appliances that were boxy yet and rounded at the corners, no microwave, no espresso machines…just a two-slice toaster and a row of cook books held up by marble bookends in the shape of futuristic space ships were on the counter.

He sat down on one of the aluminum chairs as his 'mother' poured him a cup of coffee from a silver percolator.

"Thanks." Terry sipped it.

"There's milk in the fridge." She pointed, looking slightly confused. Maybe Shannon drank his coffee with cream and sugar. Terry stood up and opened the refrigerator, seeing a glass bottle filled with milk and zero plastic containers in the interior. The shelves were stocked with 'real food'; vegetables, fruit, meat, cheese, and juice.

He removed the milk bottle and poured it into his coffee cup, though he preferred it black. While he did, his mother used a spoon to dump two sugars into it. Terry winced and tried to imagine drinking it now.

"Why did you come back, Shannon? Did you think about what your father said last night?" She cracked eggs into a cast iron skillet.

Terry sat down and watched her cook, sipping the sugary coffee and putting it down in distaste. "What did we argue about again?"

She spun around, appearing surprised.

He shrugged.

"Don't act innocent. You know what you did." She removed a bag of white bread from a counter breadbox, and put two slices into the toaster.

TiMELESS

"Remind me." Terry smelled the browning butter in the pan and his stomach grumbled.

She made a snorting sound and turned her back on him.

"Look, Mom," Terry didn't want to go back to the hotel, so he tried to make peace. "I'm sorry. Okay? I'll do whatever Dad wants me to do."

"Why the change of heart?" She glanced over her shoulder at him, spatula in hand.

"The hotel sucked."

"Language!"

"Sorry." He sipped the coffee again and cringed, pushing it away.

"Shannon, all we want is for you to succeed. You're nineteen and you need to go to college and get a good job. You can't live here forever."

"I don't want to live here forever." Terry looked around the modest home. "Am I enrolled in college?"

The bread popped up from the toaster and she buttered it. "Are you being silly on purpose?"

"No."

"Yes, you're enrolled in college. You're going part time while you work with your father at his office. Why are you acting so strangely?"

"Am I supposed to be working with him today?" Terry sat back as she served him the eggs, sunny-side-up on the white toast.

"Shannon Albright!" She sounded exasperated, putting a knife and fork on the table for him. "Why do you have to be so sarcastic?"

"I don't mean to be." Terry was starving so he ate the food hungrily.

"It's Friday. You only work with him three days a week."

"Okay." Terry ate all the food on his plate, once again trying the sweet coffee to wash it down. He pretended it was a frappe since it was cold now.

Once he had finished, she removed the plate from him and washed it in the sink. No dishwasher. "Do you want anything else, dear?"

"I'm good for now. Do you mind if I go to my room?"

Looking over her shoulder she asked, "Why would I mind?"

Terry put his mug in the sink for her to wash. He kissed her cheek from behind and said, "Thanks for breakfast."

"Well! Whatever thinking you did over the past week on your own, I'm glad you came back a different man. It is time you grew up and stopped acting like a…well…you know."

"A 'you know'?"

She shook her head and returned her focus to the dishes.

Terry didn't want to ask her which room was his, so he hunted around the lower floor. The house was very small, the rooms tiny and claustrophobic. A den, a bathroom, and a master bedroom, were the only other rooms on the bottom floor. He had spotted a staircase right inside the front entryway when he entered the house so he took the carpeted stairs two by two and stood at the top landing. There were two bedrooms in a dormer style attic, slanted ceilings which added to the claustrophobic feel. Terry poked his head into one. Clothing was piled on the floor, the bed was unmade. He checked into the second room. It was painted pink and had low pile red carpet and posters of Elvis Presley and the Beatles on the tilted walls.

"Okay. That can't be mine." He spun on his heels and entered the messy room, looking at the details. A single bed without a headboard, a matching dark wood dresser and highboy, and a bookshelf with car magazines and a few model airplanes on it, made it appear very average for a young man in his late teens.

TiMELESS

Terry opened the nightstand drawer, rummaging through the junk, finding condoms and petroleum jelly. That surprised him.

He opened drawers of his dresser; underwear, socks, T-shirts, shorts, the usual apparel for a high school or college kid.

Looking at his small bed, Terry raised the mattress. "Aha." He removed magazines and had a look. "*Beefcake*. Now I got it. Oh, the irony."

He flipped though the issue, nodding in approval at the handsome men. "Nice."

Hearing a noise, Terry hid the magazines again and stood at the landing looking down.

"Hi, Mom!" a young woman called. "Is that Shannon's car? Is he home?"

"Yes, Tammy! He's upstairs," his mother yelled to her.

Instantly Tammy spun to look up the steep narrow staircase, seeing him. "Shannon!" She barreled up the stairs to him.

He was nearly knocked off his feet by her embrace. "Was I gone that long?"

"Yes, you jerk. I missed you." She stepped back as if to inspect him and Terry did the same to her, checking out her high ponytail, a pink crew neck sweater with a white-collared lacy shirt under it, and Capri pants. Out of the side of her mouth she asked, "Did you tell them you'd go straight?"

Terry made a noise in his throat. "Is that what Dad and I argued about?"

Tammy tilted her head at him. "Are you kookie?"

"Yes?" He nodded, trying to get her to confirm his suspicions.

She held his hand and dragged him into her room, sitting on the floor in front of a low shelf with a turntable and record albums on it. He was tugged down to sit on the floor beside her. "What are you going to do about Kenner?"

"About Kenner?" Terry noticed a stack of 'forty-five' records with the plastic adapters in them. He smiled and picked one up to inspect.

"Shannon!" Tammy whacked him on the arm. "Stop being the odd ball."

"I don't know. What should I do?"

"You guys are so in love."

Terry immediately paid attention.

"What?" she asked. "You are. He's been going out of his mind since you took off. How could you not tell him where you were?"

Terry wondered without a cell phone and computer, how anyone could do anything to communicate.

"Shannon!"

"What?" Terry flinched as she hit him again.

She studied his eyes and Terry grew nervous she may figure out he might look like her brother, but…

"You caved." She folded her arms over her chest. "You caved and told dad you wouldn't see him. Am I right?"

"I didn't cave, but that hotel was crap."

"Crap? Since when do you say that?" She laughed. "Is that where you were? In a hotel?"

"I have to finish college, I have to work, Tammy."

"You turned into a punk on me? Does Kenner know you're dumping him? What are you going to do? Date girls?" She snorted like it was absurd.

"How long have you known I was gay?" Terry asked quietly.

Tammy tilted her head. "Even before you admitted it. I found the magazines in your room."

"You looked under my mattress?" he asked in surprise.

"Oh? You have good ones there?" She stood and bolted to his room.

TiMELESS

Terry raced after her and watched as she tugged the *Beefcake* issues out of their hiding spot.

"Boss! Beats the Sears catalogue."

"That's not the magazine you meant?"

"No. You used to keep all the issues of *Life Magazine* with the Marlboro man in them." She appeared enthralled with the nude men pictures.

Terry ran his hand over his head and tried to think. "So, it looks like in order to live here and have Dad pay for my college..."

"You have to stop seeing Kenner and swear off men." She glanced at him from over the magazine. "You're going to lie."

"Are we into church?"

"Huh?" She tilted her head. "Did you just ask me—"

"Never mind." He held up his hand.

"Tammy? Shannon? Do you have any dirty clothing to wash? I'm going to do a load of laundry!" their mother called from the bottom of the stairs.

Tammy hid the magazine quickly under the mattress and then shrank back. "Give her your sheets. They look like they've got cooties." She walked out of the room and into hers.

Terry pulled back the blankets to see white crusty stains on the bedding. He rubbed his face tiredly and stripped the bed.

CHAPTER 2

At six pm, Terry was relaxing on clean sheets. He had straightened up the pigsty of his room, taking the clothing his mother had washed and organizing the drawers into neatly folded stacks of his clothing. To say his mother was stunned was an understatement.

Tammy was in her room with a friend, Elvis Presley music playing loudly. Even with her door closed, it vibrated the top floor. Terry imagined her dancing to it, lip-synching the words.

The front door slammed and Terry sat up with a start. He stood at the landing and could hear his mother's voice, "Bob, calm down. Yes, Shannon is home but he's going to fly straight."

Fly straight? Terry scoffed in his throat. *Over my dead body.*

"Shannon!" was thundered loudly.

Terry scrambled down the stairs to come face to face with a man in a black business suit, white shirt, and narrow tie, dark framed glasses, clean shaven, and an ultra conservative buzz cut.

"Your mother said you understand the rules of this house." The older man sneered in distaste.

"I do." Terry met his mother's worried gaze.

"You want your college paid for?"

"Yes."

"Then you date women! You hear me?"

"Bob..." his mother shivered as if the topic repulsed her.

16

TiMELESS

The urge to battle fiercely was in Terry, but he shut up. "Okay." Terry shrugged.

"Bob, Shannon cleaned his room. You should see it. It's neat as a pin. And he mowed the lawn!"

Bob didn't appear impressed. He left the room and closed the door to the master bedroom with a slam.

"You'll be fine now." She patted Terry's arm. "Dinner will be on the table in five minutes. Let your sister know."

"Okay." He climbed the stairs and tapped the door. "Tammy?"

He heard giggling and the music lowered. The door opened and Tammy's friend, Cecilia grinned at him. "Hi, Shannon." She appeared flirty and slightly infatuated.

"Hi. Tell Tammy Mom said dinner in five." Before he walked away, Tammy said, "Come here!"

"What?" Terry wondered how long he was going to have to pretend to be Shannon and what was the point of being stuck in 1961? He had too much to do and needed to leave.

"Come here!" Tammy grabbed his shirt and dragged him into the room. "Got a plan to keep Dad off your back."

"What plan?"

"Date Cecilia!"

Terry looked at the petit blonde, who was giving him a lascivious leer. "I don't want to date anyone."

"Tammy! Dinner!" was yelled from below.

"No, Shannon, it's just a cover. You don't really have to date her."

"Unless you want to." Cecilia smiled at him eagerly.

"Tammy? Is your friend joining us?"

"No, Mom!" Tammy yelled in reply. She spoke softly. "Just a thought, big brother. In case." She held Cecilia's hand and they headed down the stairs.

"Bye, Shannon." Cecilia smiled devilishly.

"Bye." Terry walked passed Tammy as she said goodbye to her friend at the door and looked into the kitchen. His father had the newspaper in his hand and was smoking a pipe as his mother placed serving platters of food on the table and made up a plate for the old man.

Terry inhaled the sweet pipe smoke and didn't know where to sit, assuming they had traditional spots. He lingered until Tammy showed up, then let her take her place first, moving to the chair opposite his father at the table for four, leaving his mother to sit closest to the stove and sink.

His mother began passing the food to Terry.

"Thanks. It looks great." He stuck the serving fork into a piece of fried chicken and put it on his plate. Another bowl of peas and carrots was handed to him, and rolls were passed around.

Bob finally folded his paper and put his pipe down on a stand. Immediately his mother placed both items on the counter behind him, the perfect servant.

"Looks good, Carol."

"Thank you, dear." She poured juice in everyone's glass.

Terry picked up his food to eat and his mother cleared her throat loudly. Before he put the food into his mouth, Terry looked up. They were all staring at him. "What?"

"We haven't said grace." His mother elbowed him.

"Oh." *Knew it.* Terry put the fork down and his mother said, "Thank you, Lord, for this meal we are about to share."

"Amen," his father said.

Tammy didn't respond and began eating. After she chewed she said, "Dad, Shannon is going to take Cecilia out to dinner tomorrow night."

Bob raised his eyebrow suspiciously.

Terry didn't say a word, eating hungrily.

"Right, Shannon?" Tammy smiled.

TiMELESS

"Yeah. Sure."

"That's wonderful!" Carol said, "She's a lovely girl. She's going to the same college as you this September, Shannon."

He nodded, his cheeks full of food, having no idea what school it was.

"Isn't she, Bob?" Carol asked.

"Hurmph." Bob didn't appear convinced, and neither was Terry.

Terry tried not to glare at the man, and focused on his meal. When he first began this experiment with his fellow scientists and mathematicians, he had no idea he was going to get stuck in eras that had no connection to his goal. And he had no way to communicate to figure out what was going on in his own present time. This wasn't *Quantum Leap* and he had no 'Al.'

Tammy didn't finish her food and asked, "May I be excused?"

Carol pointed to her plate. "There are people starving in China."

"I'm full, Mom." She tilted her head at her father. "Daddy?"

"You're excused." He smiled at her.

Terry immediately caught the favoritism, but wasn't surprised. He was a fag while she was daddy's little sweetheart. He didn't resent Tammy for it. Not one bit. He resented 'Bob'.

As if saving him, Tammy held out her hand. "Come on, Shannon. Help me with my college applications."

He looked at his father first, and was ignored. He said to his mother, "You want me to do the dishes?"

She appeared stunned and Bob slammed his hand on the table in anger.

"What?" Terry had no clue what he did wrong.

"Come on!" Tammy grabbed his hand and dragged him off.

"Thanks for dinner," he said and nearly fell on his face Tammy was pulling so hard.

19

When they were out of hearing range, Tammy shook her head. "Do the dishes? And you want Dad to think you're not gay anymore? Sheesh!"

"I don't think it's fair. If you cook you shouldn't have to clean up too." He followed her up the stairs.

"Man, you're really messed up. Stop saying kookie stuff." She pulled him into her room and shut the door. "Okay, here's the plan for tomorrow night. You're going to take me to Cecilia's and pretend to go out on a dinner date with her."

"Okay."

"She's got a crush on you." Tammy smiled and searched through her record albums for something to play.

"I got that impression."

"Oh well. Her loss." Tammy put Roy Orbison's music on the turntable.

~

By ten his parents were in the den watching the late news, waiting for *The Tonight Show with Jack Paar*, and Tammy was in bed.

Fully dressed, Terry laid on the mattress in his room, staring at the ceiling, trying not to lose his mind as he waited to leave where he was and go where he needed to be.

A noise made him look at the window. He didn't hear anything more so he closed his eyes. A second later he heard another noise. It was a pebble hitting his window glass. He jolted upright and pushed the curtains aside. Unable to see in the dark, Terry opened the wooden sash window and looked out. Someone was waving to him from under a birch tree on the far end of the driveway.

There was no way Terry could leave through the front door unnoticed. He pulled the screen off, climbed out, and slowly made his way down the shingle-roofed garage to the eave. He could see a man waiting.

TiMELESS

Terry held the edge over the gutter and stepped down on his father's Buick, wondering if the car alarm would sound, then realized no one had car alarms in 1961. He released his hold, and hopped off the front of the car to the ground. Immediately the man raced for him, embracing him in the dark.

"Kenner?" Terry asked, assuming it had to be the forbidden fruit.

"Why did you split without telling me?" Kenner held Terry's jaw in his fingers.

About to shake his head and make something up, Terry met Kenner's gaze in the moonlight. What he saw rocked him to the core. "Sky?"

"Huh?" Kenner appeared confused. "Sky?" He looked upwards. "What about it?"

Terry grabbed Kenner's sleeve and brought him to stand under the lamppost. He inspected this man carefully, feeling chills wash over his skin. Though this gorgeous hunk was only nineteen, and didn't look exactly like...like his...

Terry couldn't catch his breath. He saw something familiar in this man's brown eyes.

"I missed you." Kenner cupped Terry's face. "How could you tune out like that and not tell me where you went? I was low, really low about it."

Terry tried to stop his thoughts, which were, *You're Sky! You're my man!* and instead, thumbed over his shoulder. "My old man was about to kill me."

Kenner looked around the quiet street, then grabbed Terry's hand and ran with him to a path between homes which cut through a cul-de-sac and into a vacant wooded lot along a main street. It was nearly pitch black without streetlights, but soon Terry's eyes adjusted to the dimness.

The minute they were hidden, Kenner cupped Terry's jaw and kissed him.

Terry went crazy. The taste, scent, even the technique of the kiss was so familiar, he didn't know if it was Shannon's senses and knowledge of his lover's touch, or his.

Kenner backed Terry up against a tree trunk and leaned on him, pressing his crotch into Terry's. The feel of that hard cock against his sent Terry reeling. "I've missed you, oh, baby, baby..." Terry clutched at Kenner tightly, tears rolling down his cheeks.

"I missed you too. How could you cop a breeze without telling me?" Kenner combed his fingers through Terry's hair.

Terry stared at Kenner, seeing Sky so clearly in him and trying to understand how this moment may make a difference to the purpose of his experiment. "You've never heard the name Sky Norwood?"

"Shannon, no. Who is he? If you met someone else, I'll flip."

"Never mind." Terry embraced him, kissing his neck and squeezing him so tight he felt their hearts beating as one.

"What did you tell your keepers?" Kenner caressed Terry's cheek.

"Keepers?"

"Your parents." Kenner tilted his head as if Terry was the one speaking a strange language.

"I had to tell them I'd stop seeing you. My dad's paying for my tuition and I work at his office."

"I know. Believe me. I'm in the same boat." Kenner kissed Terry again and the heat and passion made Terry so hot he was going out of his mind. A rush of all the moments he and Sky had ever shared nearly consumed him.

"Where did you go?" Kenner cupped the back of Terry's head, appearing worried. "You couldn't even get on the horn and tell me?"

"Some shitty motel. I don't know."

"Why didn't you let me know?"

TiMELESS

"How? With no fucking cell phone?"

"Cell phone? What's a cell phone? You mean you couldn't find a payphone?"

"Oh God." Terry's eyes kept filling with tears and he wiped them on his shirt. "I want you."

"I want you too." Kenner smiled shyly.

"Where can we go?" Terry ran his hand down Kenner's tightly packed abs to his crotch. He felt where Kenner had grown hard in his pants and rubbed him hotly.

"You're going to make me come." Kenner inhaled deeply and closed his eyes.

Terry looked around the area. "Can I suck you here?"

"Or we can do the backseat bingo." Kenner dug his fingers into Terry's hair. "What we usually do."

"Back seat? You mean a car?" Terry felt defeated. "I hate fucking in cars. I haven't done that since—" he shut up and met Kenner's confused gaze.

"Since?"

"Since last time we did it." Terry opened Kenner's belt buckle.

"You cool?" Kenner searched Terry's eyes.

Terry tugged down Kenner's zipper and stuffed his hand into his pants, rooting out his cock. Once Terry had his fingers around it, he met Kenner's gaze. He knew this dick. Knew it well.

"Shannon," Kenner said softly, "I love you so much."

Terry's passion nearly ended in him breaking down in sobs of grief. "I love you too. Oh, God, forever!" Terry cupped the back of Kenner's head through his slicked back, Elvis' style haircut, and kissed him, tears running down his face. "Miss you. Miss you," Terry said against Kenner's lips, feeling Kenner's cock throb in his fingers.

"My car?" Kenner wiped the tears from Terry's cheeks.

"Where did you park? What about cops?"

"The heat?" Kenner chuckled, touching where Terry's hand was inside his pants. "We've never gotten caught before. I'm on a side street, not in a county park."

"Okay." Terry removed his hand from Kenner's clothing and they jogged through the dim trail back to the quiet neighborhood.

A red 1959 Plymouth Fury was parked near an empty wooded lot. Kenner opened the back door and crawled in. Terry followed him, surprised at how enormous the backseat was. He lay on top of Kenner and closed the door, going for his mouth.

After hot kissing, Terry leaned up, looked around the deserted area and opened Kenner's pants again. He exposed Kenner's cock and then tugged his own pants down his legs. Once they were bare from the thighs to their waist, Terry lay back down on top of him and kept kissing Kenner, grinding their cocks together. "Do you have a rubber and lube?"

"A rubber?" Kenner laughed. "I can't get pregnant."

"No...for STDs."

"STDs?"

"Sexually transmitted diseases." Terry leaned up on his arms as they spoke.

"We never worried before. Why? Did you pick up something I don't know about?"

"Huh? No."

"What's going on, Shannon?"

"Nothing. Kiss me." Terry pushed his crotch against Kenner's, moaning softly. They swirled tongues and the fire between them grew. "I want to fuck you."

Kenner laughed wickedly. "Wow. You're really crazy tonight."

"I am. Crazy about my man." Terry kissed Kenner's neck and shifted his position so he was kneeling on the floor. "I can't believe how big this car is."

"Huh?"

"Nothing." Terry held Kenner's cock at the base and enveloped it.

"Oh, Shan. That feels so good." Kenner held Terry's head and thrust his hips upwards into his mouth.

Even the scent of Kenner's groin was familiar, everything was. Terry drew Kenner's cock deep and sucked hard, moaning as his own cock grew hungry for release. He knew how it was with him and Sky, Terry was usually the aggressor, but not exclusively. Just that he and Sky preferred it that way.

"Shannon…I'm…I'm…" he let out a low groan.

Terry knelt higher and sucked deeper, faster, pushing his hand between Kenner's legs to get to his rim. Kenner let out a surprised gasp and came, his body thrusting upward, off the seat.

Swallowing, Terry rubbed friction on the base of Kenner's cock to his ass and milked him strongly. He kissed the head of Kenner's cock and said, "I missed that. You taste fantastic."

"Did you go out on me?"

"Huh?" Terry blinked and caught Kenner's suspicious gaze.

"You never did that before."

"Did what? Sucked you off?"

"No. The…the thing you did between my legs."

Terry didn't know what to say. "I never did that? You sure?"

"Am I sure?" Kenner pulled on his soft cock.

"I…" Terry wondered how inexperienced Shannon was.

"I liked it. Just have no idea why we've never done that before."

"Have I fucked you?"

"Huh?" Kenner tilted his head. "Yes! Shannon, what's going on?"

"Nothing. I'm just a little tired."

"Then you don't want to…"

"No! I do!" Terry got to his knees, looked around at the deserted area again first and began jerking himself hard. Kenner rolled over and tugged his pants to his ankles.

"Lube?"

"Huh?" Kenner glanced at him.

"What do we use to lubricate?"

"Oh. The lotion is under the seat."

Lotion. Terry reached under the passenger's seat and located a bottle of hand cream. "It'll do."

"It's what we always use." Kenner spread his legs.

Terry used a generous amount on his cock, then pushed his slick finger into Kenner.

"Like wow."

Terry tilted his head in confusion. "Please tell me I've done this to you before."

"Not like this."

"Fuck." Terry tried to keep hard with all the distractions. *Shannon is one shitty lover.* He ran his fingers over Kenner's prostate and gave it a nice rub.

"Shannon! That's so boss!"

Terry shook his head at the absurdity. He knelt on top of Kenner and pushed his cock inside him. "Oh, that's nice."

He heard Kenner chuckle.

"You good?"

"I'm good."

Terry pushed in deeper feeling Kenner relax. He moaned and stared at his ass in the dimness of the moonlight. "Not gonna take me long."

"Good 'cause I have to bug out soon."

Terry hammered into Kenner and felt as if he were making love to Sky. As the emotion tried to wash over him, Terry kept it at bay and pushed Kenner's clothing up his back to see his body more clearly. He gave a few more thrust and came, closing his eyes.

"There it is." Kenner laughed tiredly.

Terry pulled out and stared at his dick. "You're gonna be a sticky mess."

"It's how I always am after this." Kenner shifted and pulled his pants up his legs as Terry craved a soapy washcloth or even a tissue. He tucked himself in and closed his pants.

"I gotta go before my dad suspects something." Kenner sat up on the seat.

"How will we stay in contact?"

"Meet me somewhere. Tomorrow?"

"Tammy arranged for me to have a fake date with her friend Cecilia."

"Your sister's the boss."

"Huh?" Terry sat beside Kenner on the wide bench seat.

"She's hip. I'm really cranked she did that."

Terry gave up trying to decipher the strange slang. "Yeah, she's great."

"What time?"

"How about seven?"

"Cool." Kenner nodded. "Where?"

"Name it."

"There's a place in Teaneck. Dark spot. Men only. Where we can be…ya know."

"A gay club?" Terry asked, his hand on Kenner's knee.

"Gay club?"

Terry rubbed his face. "You said it's a place we can be…ourselves?"

"Yeah. Men. All men."

About to say, text me the address, Terry stopped himself. "Where in Teaneck?

"Main Street. We went there once before."

"What's the name of it?"

"Duke's."

"See ya there at seven." Terry leaned forward for a kiss.

Kenner held him tight, then tilted his head to the door. "Have to split before I get caught."

"Me too." Terry exited the car and tucked in his shirt.

Kenner looked around and then kissed Terry quickly one last time, and got behind the wheel. He started the car and drove off, putting his headlights on after a block.

Terry headed home, trying to figure out why Kenner felt so much like Sky, and why he was here in the first place.

This wasn't an era where he could be an advocate for gay rights. Hardly. It was a generation of young people rebelling against their parents, yes, salivating over Elvis and listening to music their parents hate.

Terry began to convince himself his familiarity with Kenner's body was really Shannon's not his own.

He stood in front of his house and so far it appeared calm. He hopped on his dad's car and shimmied up the garage, low crawling to his open window. Once inside, he reattached the screen and needed a shower. It was eleven-thirty and he could hear the television on downstairs in the den. He found clean briefs and a pair of sweat pants and tiptoed down the stairs.

As he approached the bathroom in the hall, his parents were sitting in the dark, watching TV. His dad smoking his pipe, his mom knitting. Jack Paar's monologue was audible.

He opened the bathroom door and shut it behind him, turning on the light. Locking the door, he stripped and started the shower, hoping taking one at near midnight wasn't enough to again arouse suspicion.

TiMELESS

Standing under the water, looking at the pink and black ceramic tile which surrounded the tub, Terry washed and became too tired to think. He had to somehow meet Kenner in Teaneck tomorrow night, using a map as his guide and pretending he was on a date with Cecilia.

"I don't need this shit. I really don't." Terry closed his eyes and exhaled loudly.

CHAPTER 3

No! No! Oh, God please no!

"Shannon? Are you awake? Time to get up! You have chores to do!"

Terry came around from a deep sleep, drenched in sweat and waking from a horrific nightmare. He threw off the covers, burning up.

A knock came to his door. "Shannon?" The door opened and his mother stepped in. She covered his eyes and spun around. "Make yourself decent!"

Terry glanced down at his naked body and tugged the sheet over his crotch, feeling sick and feverish, drained from a nightmare that was simply a recurring memory, and not made up by his brain.

Carol peeked at him. "Since when do you sleep in the nude? Where are your pajamas?"

"I'm sick. I don't feel well." He wiped at his forehead.

She rushed over and sat on the bed, putting her hand to his forehead. "You are burning up."

"How hot is it in here?" He wiped his face with both hands. "Can't you turn on the air-conditioner?"

"The air-conditioner?" She touched his neck. "You're drenched. Shannon, it's not that hot in the house. And your father can put the fan in your window if you want."

"I'm sick. I don't feel right." Terry held his stomach.

"I'll see if Dr Rosen can come."

"Huh?" Terry narrowed his gaze on her.

"Sit tight. Don't move. Let me call him."

"I'm not moving." Terry groaned and rolled to his side.

The night-terror came back to him and he tried to shake off its effects. Below him he could hear his mother speaking to his father. "He's ill, Bob. Let me get the doctor to come over."

"Shannon?" Tammy said softly.

"What?" He didn't roll over to face her.

"You're sick?"

"Yeah." He closed his eyes.

"Anything I can do?"

He shook his head.

The sound of footfalls on the stairs came next. Terry knew by the heavy tread it must be his dad.

"Go to your room, Tammy."

"Yes, Dad."

Terry didn't face him. He felt the blanket being jerked up to cover him. Terry pushed it off. "I'm boiling. Stop."

"Put on something. What is wrong with you?"

"Mom said you had a fan?"

"It's not hot in the house. It's not even seventy."

Terry rolled to his back and squinted at his discomfort. "Why do you hate me so much?"

"I don't hate you."

"You do." Terry closed his eyes and felt a wave of dizziness.
He heard Carol's voice, "The doctor is on his way, Bob. He said twenty minutes."

"I'll wait downstairs. Make him put something on."

Terry moaned and held his temples as his head throbbed.

"Come on. Slip these on."

He tried to open his eyes and found Carol attempting to place a pair of Jockey Y-front undies on him. Terry grabbed the waistband and tugged them up. She then began bringing the sheet up.

"No. I'm hot! I'm sweating like a pig! Stop covering me and get me a fan!"

"No need to be so rude!" She left the room, returning with a wet washcloth for his head.

"Thank you. I'm sorry." Terry held it on his forehead and shook from what felt like fever chills.

"You see? Now you're cold." She covered him up.

"Why is this happening? Why? Not now."

"Let the doctor check you out."

"Are you taking me to the hospital?" Terry used the cloth on his face.

"No. He's coming here. He's on his way."

"A doctor is coming here?"

"Yes. This isn't the first time Dr Rosen has come here. Why are you so surprised?" She sat on the bed and kept checking his forehead with the back of her hand. "You are burning up."

Terry covered his face in frustration and moaned.

"Do you feel as if you're going to be ill? Do I need a pail?"

"No. Just a fan! Why is it so hot in here?"

She pushed the window sash up higher, but Terry didn't feel any breeze.

He kept still and tried to rest as she dabbed his forehead and neck with the cool cloth.

What felt like an eternity passed and he heard voices at the front door. Carol left his side and soon a man's deep voice was near him. "What seems to be the trouble?"

"I don't know, Doctor. He just woke up in a sweat and feels hot."

"Okay. Let me examine him."

TiMELESS

Terry heard his door close and tried to see, though his eyes wanted to remain closed from the pain in his head. An older man with graying temples and the same style of dark rimmed glasses as his dad approached him, carrying a medical bag and wearing a stethoscope around his neck.

"I'm going to take your temperature, Shannon."

"Okay." Terry opened his mouth.

"Roll to your stomach."

"Huh?" Terry noticed the doctor shaking the thermometer, getting the mercury down.

"Roll over, son."

"Oh Christ." Terry figured it out. He dragged his underwear down and waited as an anal thermometer was pushed into his ass with petroleum jelly. *Unbelievable.* He hid his face in the pillow, completely humiliated. *Sure. A strange guy can put something in my ass, but my lover can't. What a world.*

"How long does that thing have to be in my butt?" Terry tried to see the doctor, but all the man did was sit beside him patiently. Terry assumed the doctor knew about his preference for men. There was no doubt he was told by his father downstairs at the door. He could hear it now, it was God's way of punishing him. Wasn't that what they would say?

The anal thermometer was finally removed.

"You're running a high fever. We need to get you into a tub of cold water."

"Oh God. Why am I sick?"

The doctor reached to help Terry off the bed. Terry felt weak and shaky as the doctor tugged his underwear up to cover him.

"Bob! Can you give me a hand?" Dr Rosen called out.

Immediately Terry's dad entered the room and with a man on either side of him, Terry was helped to walk. In the tight gap of the stairs, Terry had one in front and one behind, holding him up.

33

He could hear the bathtub running as the doctor requested, and Terry was urged to get into the cool water. He tugged the underwear off, dropped them on the floor, and climbed in. The water felt wonderful and his mother brought a bucket of ice from the kitchen.

The doctor checked Terry's pulse rate first, holding his wrist and staring at his watch, then he listened to his lungs with his stethoscope.

Carol covered Terry's groin with a washcloth and said, "Tammy, don't come in!"

"Mom, I'm worried."

Dr Rosen said, "I think he's caught a bug. Though it's unusual in May, it's certainly not impossible." He wrote up a prescription. "This is for penicillin. Make sure he finishes it all. Bed rest and fluids."

"Thank you."

Dr Rosen touched Terry's shoulder. "You need to stay in bed, son. Rest." He stood and said to Terry's parents, "If the fever doesn't let up in a couple of days, call me again. But after taking the pills and bed rest he should be fine."

"Okay. Thank you."

Carol stayed behind as Bob walked the doctor to the door.

Terry moaned and stared at his submerged body, having no way to let Kenner know he was sick. Then he thought of Tammy. "Sis!"

"Yeah?"

"You're not decent!" Carol held Tammy back.

"Mom, let her come in!" Terry held the cloth over his groin.

"Why do you need her here so badly?"

"Mom!" Tammy pushed her way inside the tiny bathroom. "What, Shannon?"

"Can you tell..." He peeked at his mother. "Can you tell Cecilia I can't make it? Please. She has to know."

Timeless

"Uh...Sure." She made a face of desperation at Terry as if she couldn't do what he was asking, even though he knew they were communicating.

"Fine. Go." Carol pushed Tammy out of the room.

"Tammy!" he yelled, "Please tell her!"

"She will!" Carol tried to calm him down. "The two of them are on the telephone long enough all day. She'll tell her."

Terry closed his eyes and finally felt cool. If Tammy couldn't contact Kenner, Terry would be crushed.

"Stay there. Your father will get you your pills and I'm going to make some broth. Don't get up."

"Okay." Terry didn't think he could anyway. He stayed still, eyes closed.

A minute later, Tammy's voice was near to him. "What's Kenner's phone number?"

"I don't have it memorized. Look him up." Terry tried to open his eyes and managed to see her beside him as she sat on the close toilet seat.

"What's his last name again?"

"Huh?" Terry stared at her in agony. "You don't know?"

"No! What is it?"

Sky Norwood! Terry shook his head and felt like crying.

"Hurry, Shannon! Mom will kill me if she sees me in here."

"I don't know."

"You don't know? How can you not know your boyfriend's last name?"

"How can *you* not know it!" he yelled through clenched teeth.

"I can't call him if I can't look him up in the directory. Where does he live?"

"Oh God..." Terry hadn't a clue. "He's meeting me at seven tonight in Teaneck at a club on Main Street called Duke's. Go there."

"Go there?" She choked. "How?"

"Take my car. Don't you have your driver's license?"

"No! You know I don't yet! Why do you think I beg you for rides all the time!"

"Tammy!" their mother scolded.

"I'm leaving." Tammy exited the bathroom and Terry moaned in frustration.

"I'm making broth."

"Mom, I'm freezing." Terry tried to hoist himself out of the tub, his teeth chattering.

She rushed to get him a towel and held it for him. "Can you stand? Your father went to the pharmacy."

"Tammy!" he hollered.

"Shannon!" Carol admonished, trying to cover him with the towel.

"Mom! Let her help me. For crying out loud! Why are you so hung up on me being naked? I'm just a human being- nothing she hasn't seen."

"Oh! Shannon! Your sister has not seen a naked man before."

"Shannon! Tell Mom you know what a guy's dick looks like and get me out of this stupid tub!"

"You are going to get me grounded, nosebleed!"

"Tammy! Language!"

"Nosebleed?" Terry held the tile wall as he stood, his mother wrapping the bath sheet around him and his sister reaching to steady him. He stepped out onto the pink bathmat and held the towel to his chest. "I need something in my stomach. I'm dizzy."

"Don't you pass out!" Tammy gripped his arm. "You'll pull us both down, ya big lug!"

"Bring him to the den. We can't carry him upstairs." Carol gripped Terry around his waist, more concerned with the towel covering him, than him falling over.

TiMELESS

Tammy held Terry from the opposite side and he leaned on her heavily as they negotiated the tight spaces to the den. Terry dropped onto the spongy padding and rested his head against the window sill behind him.

"Go get him pajamas, Tammy."

Tammy raced up the stairs.

Carol kept dabbing Terry's skin to dry him. "You'll freeze now."

"I am cold. You said you made broth?"

"Oh dear!" As if she forgot it was on the stove, Carol sprinted out of the room on her June Cleaver pumps.

Tammy returned, holding out a pair of flannel pajamas.

Terry pushed the towel off and took them as Tammy spun around, giving him her back.

He felt weak and struggled but got the bottoms on and then said, "Kid, help me with the damn top."

Tammy rushed to his side and held the pajama top for him to put his arms through. "I have never seen you this sick. What the hell is going on, Shannon?"

"I have no idea. I feel like I'm going to die." He tried to button the top but couldn't, closing his eyes and resting his head on the sofa back.

Tammy fastened his buttons for him and he heard his mother say, "Open a snack tray for him, dear."

Terry tried to see but it was a struggle. A tray table was set up and his mother put a bowl of soup on it, sitting beside him holding out the spoon. Terry reached for it but it shook out of his hand.

"Mom!" Tammy said in panic as she watched.

"Okay, calm down." Carol held the spoon up to Terry. "Open your mouth."

Terry did and she fed him the broth. At being so helpless he started crying. He heard Tammy let out a wail of anguish and her footsteps rushing away.

"Sit up," Carol spoke softly and Terry felt her trying to place a pillow behind his back.

He leaned forward for her. "I'm sorry. I'm so sorry to be this much trouble."

"Shannon. You are my baby boy. You are not trouble. Here. Take more broth."

Terry opened his mouth and tasted the salty liquid. It was like honey to him. He reached for the spoon and held it tight. "Let me try."

Carol held the spoon with him.

Terry managed to get it to his mouth without shaking the liquid off. "I have never been this ill. I'm sorry."

"Stop apologizing. This is what a mother is for."

Terry stared at her. "What is a father for?"

"He's the one getting you your medication."

"Thank you."

"Shannon..." Her eyes teared up. "This is what parents are for."

Terry held her hand and kissed it. "Parents are supposed to love their children unconditionally."

Carol sniffled and cupped the spoon to give him more broth.

Terry didn't allow her to feed him yet. "No matter what. If I die, will you remember me as the son you loved or the fag you hated?"

"Shannon!" Carol began to sob. "You're not dying."

"Answer me!"

"I love you. No matter what you do."

Terry slouched on the sofa as she brought the spoon closer to his lips. He swallowed the broth and said, "Remember this. Remember this moment. Because both you and Dad will regret everything when I'm gone."

Carol dropped the spoon and hugged him, crying. "You're not going to die. So stop saying that."

TiMELESS

Terry closed his eyes and tried not to shiver from the fever chills. A blanket was laid over him, and he fell asleep.

G. A. HAUSER

CHAPTER 4

Kenner leaned against the brick wall of Duke's, waiting. He checked his watch and ran his hand back through his hair. While men walked passed him, into the club, Kenner caught many gazes. He grew impatient and bent his knee, resting the soul of his shoe on the wall behind him. As someone drew near, Kenner asked, "You have a smoke?"

A young man in black slacks and jacket, his hair greased back, not only handed Kenner a cigarette, he lit if for him. "You get cranked?"

"Don't know. So far, he's just late." Kenner took a puff of the cigarette.

"My boys and me will buy you a drink." The young man gestured to the group behind him.

"Yeah. Cool." Kenner glared at the passing cars, as if they were Shannon, and entered the dark club with his new friends.

~

Terry swallowed his third penicillin tablet with orange juice. He kept checking the clock as he sat in the den with his parents, watching *My Three Sons* on TV. Tammy was out with Cecilia and no one commented that Cecilia didn't even ask Terry about their supposed 'date' this evening.

TiMELESS

"I want to go to bed." Terry's chills had subsided, but he felt weak.

"Bob, help Shannon." Carol put her knitting aside.

"I can do it." Terry stopped his dad from getting up. Slowly, Terry made it to his feet, using the wall and then the open door of the room to keep upright. He heard his parents say something behind him in hushed tones, but all of Terry's thoughts were of getting out and meeting Kenner.

He climbed the stairs with a hand on either wall. Once he was in his room, he removed the pajamas and dressed, struggling with waves of dizziness and chills. He hoisted the pants up, tucked his wallet into his pocket and picked up his car key. Battling with feeling completely off and wondering if he had the flu as Shannon or something was going wrong with the experiment, Terry sat on his bed.

After he put his shoes on, he stuffed rolled up blankets with his duffle bag and clothing to make it look like there was someone in the bed sleeping.

He pushed out the screen, leaned it against the window, and shimmied down the garage roof.

~

Kenner lit up another cigarette as a live band played the new Chubbie Checker's hit, *Pony Time*. It was so loud, he couldn't hear the guy next to him talking. Another round of booze was brought to the table and he held up his shot of vodka and tapped the other glasses as they rose for the toast.

Kenner tossed the booze down and wiped his mouth with the back of his hand, choking on the burn and completely drunk.

He was stuck. Stuck loving someone he could not be caught loving, and then losing him again and again.

Why did Shannon keep leaving him? Not meeting him?

His eyes burned with his tears but he held them back and sucked another puff of the cigarette, blowing the exhale into the already smoke-filled room.

One of the men tapped him. "We're going to New York to hit a club. You in?"

"No. Thanks." Kenner finished one last shot of vodka and snuffed out the cigarette in a tin ashtray. He was left alone at the table and stared at the live band in a daze, sinking emotionally from the thoughts in his head.

Fed up, furious that Shannon did not show, Kenner stood from the table, knocking into it as he swayed. He made his way into the night air, through a crowd of men who were lingering on the sidewalk out front, smoking.

Stuffing his hand into his pocket, he removed his car key, and staggered down the block, looking for his car.

~

Trying to navigate the unfamiliar highway system without his satellite navigator, Terry had the map unfolded on the passenger's side of the bench seat, and the dome light on. He drove east on Route 4 and left the highway at Teaneck, feeling sick and sweaty from a fever. He finally found a sign for Main Street and slowed down.

Blue and red lights were flashing, throwing colors on the glass and metallic surfaces around the street. A fire truck and several police cars were blocking the road. Terry approached slowly in the tied up traffic as a cop directed them away from what appeared to be an accident. As he crawled by, Terry could see a red Plymouth Sport Fury's front end, wrapped around an enormous oak tree, the engine steaming and the headlights still lit and pointing in odd directions.

His heart felt as if it were in his throat. "No! No!" Terry pulled his car into a driveway and leapt out, feeling his knees weaken and his skin crawl. Four firemen were carrying a cot with a blanket covering a body away from the wreckage.

"Sky! Oh, my God! Sky!" Terry sprinted towards the victim but a cop held him back.

"Where do you think you're going?"

"Please! Is that Sky? I mean, Kenner?" Terry began to shake with chills.

"We don't know who it is."

"Please. Let me see him. Please."

The cop looked over his shoulder. "You wait here."

Terry nodded, trying not to sink to his knees from the shock and panic. As the cop left to talk to someone near the victim, Terry began to cry. "This doesn't make sense. Why am I here? I did nothing to prevent this. Why am I here?"

The cop returned and gestured for Terry to come closer. "You think you know this guy?"

Terry bit his lip and nodded.

He was brought over to the waiting firemen, all looking grim.

The police officer told Terry, "He's messed up. You sure you're ready?"

No! Terry nodded again, about to explode from helplessness.

The sheet was raised and Terry dropped to his knees and covered his face.

A fireman crouched beside him and held him. "What's his name?"

"Kenner."

The fireman nodded to his co-workers. "Then it is the guy whose ID we found."

Terry began to pass out, sliding out of the fireman's embrace. Through dulling senses, he caught the sound of men shouting for help and then everything went dark.

CHAPTER 5

Terry opened his eyes.

"Quit bogarting the weed, Dan."

He blinked and realized he was holding a lit joint. He handed it to the man beside him and looked up at the dark sky. Drizzle was falling and the unmistakable landmark of the Space Needle in Seattle was looming over him from behind a building.

Though it was cool and damp, he could tell it was not winter. No biting cold wind, but certainly a chill in the night air. But in Rain City, that could even be August.

He was handed back the joint and stared at the young man beside him. Absolutely stunning, long hair, dark brown eyes and a jaw line like Jim Morrison. He peeked down at his own clothing for a clue of where he was in time. Skin-tight jeans, Frye boots, a light denim jacket and a tight T-shirt with a Pink Floyd *Dark Side of the Moon* logo on it.

"Aren't you going to take a hit?"

Terry shook his head. "I'm stoned enough." He gave it back to this gorgeous stud. "I don't even know what year it is...uh, *dude*?" He said the last word hoping it fit the current slang.

The young man took one more hit and laughed, squeezing the joint out in his fingers. He reclined on the building beside Terry,

TiMELESS

leaning against his shoulder, staring at the illuminated Space Needle.

"No. Seriously." Terry nudged his companion. "Uh, nineteen-seventy-five?"

"You're funny as hell." This stud gave him a sexy smile.

"Christ, I hope we're lovers." Terry's cock grew thick in his pants.

The young man cracked up with laughter and seemed to find the comment hilarious.

"Are we?" Terry asked, touching his friend's thigh.

"Man, you are high." He shook his head and kept laughing.

Terry ran his hand over his own hair, feeling thick, long 'rock-star' locks. He looked at the color in the dim light; brown. He wished he had a mirror but judging by the clothing he assumed he was in his twenties. And so was his friend.

Terry was so turned on by the man, he took a chance. Cupping this hunk's face he brought his jaw towards his and kissed him lightly.

A low moan came from the handsome man and he slowly pushed Terry to lie back on the tarmac and moved on top of him, grinding their crotches together.

"Oh yes," Terry said against his lips.

The sound of a shoe scuffing the ground made them both look up.

"You two can't wait?"

Terry's partner sat up, leaning against the wall again.

"Ya got a joint, Paul?" the newcomer asked.

Paul. Terry registered his partner's name.

Paul handed the young man the rest of the joint and stood, reaching to hoist Terry up with him. "Where's the party, John?"

"Just on the other side of the Science Center. I can't remember the address, that's why I had you meet me here." He lit up the joint and puffed it.

Terry was so attracted to Paul he reached for his hand to hold as they went. Paul smiled at him and held it tightly as they walked with John.

The drizzle was mild and not drenching, and judging by the cars that drove passed at the base of Queen Anne Hill, Terry indeed thought he had come close with the year. A blue Pinto was parked in front of a red GMC Pacer. He shook his head at the sight of the classic seventies icons.

John reached to pass the joint be neither he nor Paul took it.

"Whose house are we going to?" Terry asked Paul, releasing his hand and holding him around the waist, stuffing his fingers into the back pocket of his skin-tight jeans.

"Dunno. John? Who's this chick again?"

"Got me. Just an open invite to come hang." John inhaled the smoke and blew it out, crushing the joint as they crossed a main street. "Gotta watch for the pigs." He scanned around.

"Why is pot illegal?" Paul shook his head. "I will never get that."

"Screw it," John said, "the fucking government is run by commie douchbags."

Terry smiled and felt like saying 'wait five decades, it will be.'

As Paul walked, Terry felt his ass flex and was growing so horny he was sure the minute he could he would attack this hunk.

With a tilt of his head John gestured to a door on the bottom floor of a three story brick apartment building. He tapped it with his knuckle and the minute it opened, Terry could smell marijuana and incense overwhelming the interior.

John said, "Julie told us there was a party."

A woman stepped back to allow them entry. "She's here...come in."

TiMELESS

Once Terry was inside the small apartment he could see it was lit by black lights, and day-glow posters were everywhere; Jimi Hendricks and Janis Joplin, Jim Morrison and Led Zeppelin. Peace signs and marijuana leaves glowed like neon lights from where the posters were thumb-tacked to the walls. Anyone in white was illuminated to a glowing purple, making the whole room feel animated, like a cartoon.

What Terry estimated to be around a dozen or more people were either sprawled out on the shag carpet and enormous pillows and beanbag chairs or on a low L-shaped sofa. Bodies crammed together, passing a bong.

The Eagles *Take it to the Limit* was playing loudly on the stereo. No introductions, no names exchanged by anyone in the premise, Terry stood idly as John seemed to find people he recognized. Terry leaned on Paul. "You know anyone here?"

"Nope."

"Where can we go to make out?" Terry asked, running his hand over Paul's ass.

After a laugh in amusement, Paul replied, "Anywhere?" then elbowed Terry to look at the few straight couples already engaged in heavy petting while sitting on furry throw pillows on the shag rug.

Terry wanted to explore the layout, *and* a mirror. He whispered in Paul's ear, "Have to pee. Don't go anywhere."

Paul laughed softly but Terry couldn't hear it over the music, only see his smile.

"Anyone know where the bathroom is?" Terry asked.

One person pointed to the hall.

Nodding, Terry inspected the lava and fiber optic lamps as he went, shaking his head at this strange era in humanity.

He peeked into a room. It was dark but Terry could tell it was a bedroom and someone was screwing in it. Male grunting and a woman's moans were audible. Continuing on this way, he pushed back a door and located the bathroom.

Immediately Terry shut the door behind him and turned on the light, staring into his reflection. "Damn!" He touched his face and ran his fingers through his long shaggy hair. His own blue eyes gazed back at him and he admired how adorable he was. "No wonder I got my hands on that hunk! Look at me." He peeked at his own ass in the reflection. "Oh, that does not say Jordache." He laughed in amusement. He parted his denim jacket and raised his T-shirt up to see his hairless chest, ripped abs and slim build. Pulling open his jeans he had a look at the equipment. A perfect cock, cut, and maybe six inches, or a bit more. Very nice. He stood at the toilet and relieved himself when the door opened.

Jerking his head in surprise at the intrusion he caught a woman's tipsy smile and her admiration of his physique.

"Nice bod! Wanna do it?" she said, her eyes red from either being stoned or the smoky room, and her hair was long and frizzy, tied back with a scarf.

Terry tucked his cock into his jeans and flushed the toilet, washing his hand and again catching his good looks in the mirror.

She shut the door behind her and picked up her gauzy peasant blouse, showing off her breasts.

"I…" Terry pointed to the door behind her. "I'm taken. I'm with someone."

"She can join us." The woman moved closer.

Terry nearly fell into the bathtub behind him and held onto the towel bar. "*He* not she. Nope. Gotta go." He held her shoulders, spun her around to switch places and escaped. Before he returned to the living room, he stood next to a fish tank with its glowing florescent light and removed his wallet to inspect his ID. Dan A. Whitehall, born in 1951. So, if this was the mid seventies, he was in his twenties. His address was local, Harvard Avenue East, Seattle.

TiMELESS

He had cash; a few twenties and singles, and even a credit card. He was impressed with the young man he occupied assuming him to be responsible. He tucked his wallet back into his pants and checked his pockets. Squeezing his hand into the front of his obscenely tight jeans, he tugged out a key chain with a peace sign logo attached. One key was embossed with 'Ford', the others appeared to be house keys, and maybe even a bicycle lock key. "Christ, do I own that Pinto?"

"Squeeze me."

"Huh?" Terry looked up and put his keys away.

Another wildly dressed young woman was smiling flirtatiously at him. "I said squeeze me, but I just need to get by you to the bathroom."

"Oh." He smiled. "Someone's in there."

The young woman nodded and stared at Terry dreamily. "Wanna make out?"

"I'm with…" Terry pointed over her shoulder and as he did, Paul appeared, smiling devilishly. "Him."

She spun around to see Paul. "Oh. Cool. Gay is cool."

"Damn, this beats the fucking early sixties," Terry muttered, "Hello sexual revolution!" He dove on Paul and kissed him.

Paul hugged him tight rocking him in his arms as Peter Frampton's *Show Me The Way*, came blasting out of the living room stereo.

"There's a bedroom we can mess around in," Terry said, pressing his lips against Paul's, grinding his cock into his. "Unless we have our own place. Do we?"

Paul chuckled and met Terry's eyes. "That weed really got to you. Do you have amnesia or are you fucking with me?"

Terry wedged his hand down the front of Paul's skin-tight jeans. "I wanna be fucking you."

"Where's the room?" Paul looked down the hall.

49

"It may be occupied." Terry held his hand and led him into the dark bedroom. He stopped short at the sound of the bed springs creaking, like someone was getting a good fucking.

"Ocupado." Paul tugged Terry back.

"Do I live with my parents?" Terry wanted Paul, obsessively, going out of his mind for him.

Paul cupped Terry's jaw and met his eyes, studying him as if he was truly worried Terry wasn't making sense.

It was then Terry could see Paul's inner being, like he was looking into his soul. *Sky.*

"It's you." Terry held onto Paul's face. "God damn it! It's you!"

"Did you take some ludes or something?"

Terry whispered very softly, "Sky?"

"Never heard of it. Is it an upper or a downer?"

"Shit." Terry tried to hide his disappointment. "Where can we go?"

"We just got here. Chill." He held Terry's hand and they returned to the living room, where Paul found them a spot on the shag rug beside the sofa. Leaning against the wall, holding hands, Terry had a look around at the crazy outfits of platform shoes, bell bottoms, and tie-dyed tops. And hair! Everyone in the room had a full head of long, crazy hair. It was as if he were watching the Broadway musical and someone was going to break out singing *The Age of Aquarius*.

The songs kept changing since it sounded as if the radio was tuned to a local radio station, and now ELO's *Evil Woman* was playing. While someone on the sofa tried to engage Paul in a conversation, Terry ran his hand up Paul's muscular thigh, so hot for him he was about to cream his jeans.

Seeing Paul's dimples as he smiled, his long shaggy mane of hair framing his face, Terry could recognize Sky in him and tried to figure out how that was possible. All he wanted to do when this

TiMELESS

experiment started was go back to one day. One day! Not leap around decades like a confused frog.

The bong was passed Paul's way. He took a hit and choked as he did. He was about to hand it to Terry, then said as he coughed, "No. You're already too high." He gave it back to the woman on the couch.

The door to the apartment opened and five young men entered, boisterous and rowdy, holding shopping sacks from Safeway. After they shut the door behind them, they handed out beer and bags of potato chips, crackers, and dried beef sticks, and everything else a pot smoker with the munchies would crave.

When the carrier bag was handed around for everyone to make a selection, the receipt fell out onto the floor. Terry reached for it, trying not to be too obvious he wanted to see it, and squinted in the dim light for the date. August 12, 1976.

"Son of a bitch." Terry shook his head at being pretty accurate in his guess, considering how long ago that era was from even his birth year.

Seeing everyone tossing money at the guys who supplied food and booze, Terry removed a five from his and as Paul went to open his wallet, Terry intentionally knocked it out of Paul's hand. He picked it up, smiling. "Sorry," and opened it quickly to read the driver's license. Paul B. Stevens, born in 1950, local, an address on Federal Avenue. They either did not live together, or...someone had not updated their driver's license information.

"What are you doing?" Paul laughed as he reached for his wallet.

"Sorry. Here." He gave it back to Paul who handed the man collecting cash some bills. In exchange, Paul was given a can of beer.

Seeing the big name label, Terry knew the whole microbrew generation had come much later. Paul opened the pop-top and it hissed. He took a sip and handed it off to Terry.

Just as Terry took a drink of the beer, one of the newcomers put an eight-track cassette into the stereo and *Whole Lotta Love* by Led Zeppelin blasted loudly. The crowd began dancing and singing to the lyrics.

In the chaos, Terry dove on Paul, pinning him to the floor, reaching to the corner of the room to get rid of the beer, freeing his hand. He straddled Paul and sucked on his lips and tongue, grinding on Paul's stiff cock under him. The familiarity hit Terry hard. The taste of the low quality beer, the scent of Herbal Essence shampoo in Paul's hair, his feel, his tightly packed body, Terry was going out of his mind for him.

Paul dug his fingers into Terry's hair and deepened the kiss. As if he were a school boy who could not control his body, Terry was on the verge of a climax he was so hot from Paul's touch.

"Wanna fuck you, wanna fuck you..." Terry kissed Paul between sentences, grinding on him.

Paul broke the kiss and peeked behind Terry. "Let's do it."

Terry got to his feet and hauled Paul up by his hand. Just as Terry assumed they would leave and go...somewhere...Paul wove his way through the rowdy dancing bodies to the bedroom. As they entered, a couple who had just screwed were getting dressed.

Paul thumbed over his shoulder, indicating for them to leave. "We're up."

They didn't react, simply continued straightening their appearance and left. Paul shut the door and started undressing.

"Yes!" Terry raced him to be naked. Dropping his clothing in a pile by the bed and looking at Paul as his body was revealed. He turned on the light, not wanting to miss this sight.

"Man!" Paul reacted to the brightness, dropping his pants down his legs and shielding his eyes at the same time. "What are you doing?"

"Seeing you. Damn!"

TiMELESS

"Shut that fucking thing off- you're blowing the high."

"No. Please. Wait." Terry stood before Paul and inspected him from head to toe.

"What do you mean, seeing me? Christ, you know how many times we've been naked?"

"Never enough." Terry dropped to his knees and took Paul's cock into his mouth. Memories of Sky flooded over him; his scent, his taste...

"Shut the light! I don't want some stoner chick seeing you sucking my fucking dick."

Terry had a last look up and down Paul's perfect body, then reached to the wall switch and crawled back on his knees.

"Get on the bed. Man, you are on something whacky. I'm surprised you can get it up."

The minute Paul sat down on the disheveled bed, Terry latched onto him, sitting on Paul's lap, connected to his mouth and sucking his tongue. Once they were kissing wildly, Terry gripped both their cocks pressing them together.

Paul moaned and held onto Terry's shoulders, falling back on the bed.

"Rubbers...lube?" Terry said, panting, about to come he was so hot for this man...his man.

"Dunno...check around."

"Damn! You don't have them?" Terry ground his hips on Paul's, sensing he wasn't going to need penetration to come. He was already riding the edge humping this hunk.

"Uh uh...we never use nothin'."

"Oh." Terry sat up on Paul and looked down at him while pinching his nipples.

The door opened behind them. Paul yelled, "Later!"

"Oops!" the door closed quickly.

G. A. HAUSER

"I want to suck your cock." Paul used both hands to pull on Terry's length.

"You into sixty-nine?"

"Why do you keep asking stupid questions? Get your dick up here."

Terry pivoted around and knelt over Paul's torso, going for Paul's cock. He felt his sink into a hot, warm mouth and groaned with his own mouth full. He tried to focus on his task as Paul showed just how good he was at sucking dick. It took nothing. Nothing to push Terry over the edge. He arched his back and came, closing his eyes as he held Paul's cock at the base and savored his climax. Paul milked him strongly, then bent his knees and straddled as if coaxing Terry to get back to business.

Terry waited until the waves subsided then he stare at Paul's body in delirium. "I am going to devour you."

"You talk big."

Terry scrambled to get off the bed, knelt on the floor and burrowed between Paul's thighs.

"Holy shit, Whitehall!" Paul thrust his hips off the bed as Terry lapped the base of Paul's cock and wet his rim with saliva. Once it was good and slick, he pushed his finger in and enveloped one ball at a time as he pumped Paul's dick.

"Dan! Holy Christ!"

Terry went for the head of Paul's cock and while pushing inside him he jerked him off into his mouth. Paul released a low moan and his body tensed up, his cock hard as marble. Taking the load of cum, Terry whimpered as he swallowed, urging more out of his lover. Making Paul writhe on the bed and clench his fists, Terry didn't stop until he couldn't get another drop out of Paul's slit. He wiped his mouth with his forearm and held Paul's cock in one hand. "I want you forever."

Paul chuckled, his hand on his heart.

54

TiMELESS

"I mean it!"

"You have me. What the hell are you talking about?"

Terry crawled up Paul's body to be face to face, their softening cocks nestled together. "You know we're soul mates."

"How sick am I of that fucking phrase?"

"I mean it. No matter where I go, we're together."

"Dude. What did you ingest? 'shrooms?"

A bang was heard at the door. "You guys taking forever to come?"

"Yeah, hang on!" Paul yelled and made a move to get up.

"Wait. Look at me." Terry forced Paul to stare into his eyes.

Paul appeared to think it was silly but did. "I'm looking at you. Damn you're cute."

"No. Into my eyes."

"Are you going to hypnotize me?" He laughed.

"I'm serious. Look into my fucking eyes!"

Paul's expression became stern.

They locked gazes.

"Can you see me? Can you see who I am?"

"Dude! Are you on LSD?"

"Paul!" Terry shook him. "Concentrate."

Paul let out a loud exhale and again, stared at Terry.

"Do you see me?" Terry could see Sky so clearly in Paul's eyes.

"What am I looking for? Christ, I wish I had your blue eyes."

"I love you. I will love you forever."

"Sappy! Come on, Dan. Let's get dressed before one of those stoner chicks wants a three-way."

"Do you love me?" Terry shook Paul, dying that Paul could not see the real soul behind his eyes.

"Of course. You're the best thing that's ever happened to me. You know I do."

"How long are you guys going to be in there?" came an exasperated male voice from outside the door.

Paul shifted to get off the bed, finding his clothing in the dimness. "Get dressed, ya dork."

Trying to find his clothes in the pile, Terry was so distracted by Paul getting dressed he put his leg in the wrong pant leg, making Paul laugh.

"Do we live together? Do we?" Terry asked as he managed to get his jeans on and the zipper closed over his crotch.

"No! What the hell? Dan, you're freakin' me out. Stop it. Christ, I feel like I'm in love with a zombie whose brain has been hit with electrodes." Paul tucked in his shirt and more pounding came at the door. "Come in, ya horny fuckers."

The door swung open and a couple stood at the threshold. "Let's go!" the young man gestured impatiently.

Paul left the room, looking slightly upset at the confusing messages Terry was giving off. Terry finished getting dressed, stepping into his boots and pulling the tight ankles of the jeans down over them. He hustled out of the room and watched Paul throwing back a shot of some type of hard liquor. He raced across the room. "No. Don't drink that."

Paul had already shot it down. "Don't drink what?" He laughed as he coughed on the booze.

"I'm driving." Terry pointed to himself.

John, who was obviously high or drunk, said loudly, "Is that what you said in the bedroom? Hey, which one of you plays the woman?"

Paul held his cup out for another shot. John obliged, tipping more Southern Comfort into his paper cup.

"Paul? Don't drink and drive. Ever hear of that slogan? Have a designated driver? All out there in the future somewhere?" Terry put his hand on his hips.

TIMELESS

"You're a real downer tonight, babe." Paul shook his head and said to John, "I swear, if I didn't just suck his cock, I'd say I didn't know who he was."

"You sucked his cock?" John recoiled then looked from Paul to Terry. "Wow. At first the thought was kind of gross, dude. But the two of you? You're like two stars from a rock band. Dude!" John pumped his fist as if he had an epiphany. "Let's form a band! You can be the next Deep Purple!"

Paul tossed the booze down his throat, crushed the paper cup and threw it onto a coffee table, then played 'air guitar' to the loud Manfred Mann's Earth Band's *Blinded By the Light*.

John screamed the lyrics, off key, making Terry cringe.

Someone turned on a white strobe light and the flashing bulb was painfully bright to Terry. He covered his eyes and tugged on Paul. "Let's go. I want to go home."

"Go. I'll call ya tomorrow." Paul kept jamming on his invisible guitar.

"Come with me." Terry pulled on his arm.

"It's too early, dude. Hang out. Go suck on a bong. You're freakin' me out!" Paul shouted over the noise.

Terry's head began to hurt, his ears ringing from the flickering light. The crowd in the tiny apartment had swelled to the point where it was a crush of bodies. With the noise and the pot smell, there was no way the cops wouldn't be alerted to the disturbance sooner or later.

"Paul! I'm not leaving without you!"

"Then, you're not leaving!" Paul shook his head of glorious hair as he jammed on his air guitar and yes, indeed, looked like a rock star.

Terry was so enamored by him, his jaw dropped, but he wanted Paul to leave, not to drink anymore, and certainly not to get arrested for dope.

G. A. HAUSER

There was only one thing Terry could do. Take drastic seventies action.

TiMELESS

CHAPTER 6

While standing directly in front of Paul, Terry began stripping off his clothing, folding it into a pile.

"What are you doing?" Paul's brown eyes widened.

"You going to streak?" John cheered. "Yeah! Yeah!" He kicked off his shoes and tugged his shirt up his hairy beer belly.

As Terry got naked, Paul gaped at him in amazement. When all of his clothing was off, Terry held onto it with his boots and dared him. "Ya comin' ya wimp?"

A few other young men whooped it up and began stripping down to their birthday suit while the women cheered and whistled, egging them on.

As if not able to resist the dare, Paul began shedding his clothing.

Terry held his in front of his groin as the sight of Paul nude got him rising to the occasion once more. Once Paul had his garments in his arms he nodded. "All right, Whitehall! Now what?"

"Open the damn door!" Terry yelled.

Someone obliged and Terry dashed out into the darkness, the drizzle chilling his skin, and ran towards the main street. He could hear the shrieking behind him of the others and had no idea what he was doing, but it was better than seeing Paul get drunk.

The lights of the big intersection of Queen Anne Ave and Blaine Street looked intimidating. Taking a chance that a new direction would be slightly less formidable, Terry veered off the main street and noticed a dark park and play area.

"No! Dude!" John hollered, "Let's hit the main street!"

Not gonna happen. Terry body slammed Paul, making him drop his clothing. Before Paul knew what hit him, Terry gathered it up and took off running.

Paul chased after him, laughing so hard, Terry wondered just exactly how drunk or high Paul was. This ordeal was horrifying him and Terry expected to come face to face with a Seattle cop and get arrested for lewd conduct.

"Dan! Come on! That's not funny!" but Paul kept laughing.

Once he was in the darkness of the park, and then realized there was a school there as well, Terry stopped and said, "Get dressed," shoving the clothing at Paul.

Panting to catch his breath, Paul asked, "Did you just do this to get me alone?"

"Duh!" Terry dressed, shaking he was so paranoid someone would see him.

"Come on, Dan." Paul's voice lost its humor and he put his clothing back on, struggling in the dark to see.

"Paul. You said you love me."

"Yeah, but tonight you're smothering me like a fucking needy chick." Paul tugged his shirt over his head and sat on the wet grass to put his shoes on.

"I need you. I need you to go home safe tonight."

Paul glared at him. "You are a fucking buzz kill!" He stood and put his jacket on.

"Where are you going?" Terry hopped trying to put on his boots.

"Back to the party. I thought this was supposed to be fun. It ain't!"

"Sky! I mean, Paul, wait." Terry raced after him.

Paul threw up his hands in frustration. "Go home. I'll call ya tomorrow."

"No. It can't end like this." Terry gripped Paul's arm.

"It isn't ending unless you don't cut this shit out!" Paul jerked his arm away from the grip.

"What if I told you you're going to die tonight?"

"Get the fuck away from me." Paul stormed across the grass, heading in the direction of the party.

Terry jumped on his back and put him in a headlock.

"Dan! What the fuck?" Paul grabbed Terry's arm and they wrestled.

Terry struggled to hang on, since Paul was more muscular than he was.

"You're gonna make me hurt you!" Paul warned, forcing Terry off his back.

"Nothing will hurt me more than losing you again."

"Again?" Paul wrenched free and was breathing fire as he faced Terry. In warning Paul pointed a finger into his face. "I never hurt you before. You're full of shit. I didn't even cheat. You know how many times I've been asked?"

"A lot. Look at you." Terry shook his head.

"Not once did I touch anyone! Not even a kiss!"

"Paul...listen to me." Terry stepped closer slowly. "What if I told you I wasn't really Dan?"

Paul's expression contorted at the absurdity. "Go home and sleep off the bad dope." He started walking away.

Terry grabbed his arm and made Paul look at him. "What if I told you I was from our future, yours and mine? But not as who we are now, as we—"

"Shut the hell up!" Paul shook his head. "Man, you are freakin' me out so bad tonight. All I wanted to do is hang with some friends and you're acting like you're a lunatic." He stormed off.

"You're going to be Sky Norwood! I'm Terry Lennox…listen to me!" Terry raced after him.

Paul drew back as if he was going to punch Terry, looking wild.

Terry flinched and held up his hands in defense.

Taking a few deep breaths, Paul lowered his arm and said, "Go home."

"Paul…"

"Go home!" Paul kept walking.

"I don't even know where I parked!"

Paul shook his head, not turning around.

Terry followed at a distance. The minute they rounded the corner of the block, he could see two police cars with their overhead lights rotating and John and three other guys, naked, getting arrested.

In surprise, Paul spun back to look at Terry. Terry shrugged and said, "They'll raid the party too." He noticed Paul hesitate.

Terry raced towards him, hope renewed in him. "Right? All that dope? You don't want a criminal record. That way when you graduate…"

Paul gave Terry an exasperated look.

"Uh, when your boss finds out? Did we already graduate college?"

"Go home!" Paul threw up his hands.

"I need you! Can't you see I'm all fucked up tonight? Paul. Please."

Shaking his head as he went, Paul didn't look back, returning to the Seattle Center from where they'd first come.

Following at a distance, Terry's heart was breaking. How was he supposed to accomplish this task? It was impossible.

Paul unlocked the door of a Chevy Impala and started it up. Terry stood at his driver's window, his hands on the glass, pleading.

Paul exhaled in annoyance and rolled the window down. "That's your damn car right behind me. Okay? Sheesh, Dan, sleep it off."

TiMELESS

"And you'll let me drive home even if you think I'm on something?"

"Bye." Paul pulled out of the parallel parking space, leaving Terry to shiver in fear as he watched.

He looked at the car Paul had indicated was his and figured it would be. Sitting behind the wheel of his Pinto, Terry put the key into the ignition and heard it click a few time as if the battery were low. It started after a few tries and Terry struggled to keep Paul's car in sight through his watery eyes and the bad rubber on the windshield wipers moving the damp mist.

He swiped at his eyes with his sleeve, merged into the traffic to attempt following him and soon got lost. Having no idea where Federal Ave or Harvard Avenue were, he had to pull over. He opened the glove compartment. No map.

"Fuck!" Terry rested his head on the steering wheel and tried to contain his upset. He drove around aimlessly until he located a gas station, biting his lip on his emotion. He entered the convenience store area and asked the clerk, "Can you direct me to Federal Avenue?"

"Capitol Hill?"

Terry shrugged. "Is there another Federal Ave?"

"There's a Federal Way, south of Seattle. Do you mean the town or the street?" The man pointed to a rack. "There's a map. Buy one and I'll show you both."

"No. In Seattle, not another town." Terry picked up the map and paid for it, waiting as the man pointed out the directions for him.

Starting to feel ill, Terry drove the dark wet streets up steep roads and under the interstate. He cruised along Broadway and investigated the retail shops and restaurants. Dick's Drive-In was packed with cars filled with young people eating in the parking lot, leaning against their 70's tricked out machines.

Finally Terry located the correct street. Slowly he cruised down it, looking for Paul's car. When he came to the end of the street, he turned around and began to feel that sense of doom lurking. Another pass of the glistening wet road and he did not see Paul's Chevy Impala. He parked and wished he'd written the house number down when he spied his ID.

Turning on the dome light, he checked the map to make sure this was the only Federal Avenue in Seattle, and there wasn't another he had missed.

In frustration he punched the steering wheel and rubbed his eyes. If Paul had driven home, then he should have arrived first. Maybe he parked inside a garage. What was Terry supposed to do? Bang on doors at one in the morning and see where he lived?

He gave up. Taking his driver's license out again, Terry read his own address and put the car in drive, cruising Broadway once more, to his own home, on Harvard Avenue. He was stunned it was five minutes away from Paul's street.

Parking was rough, since there was no garage or lot, and it was then he noticed an apartment number listed with his driver's license address. A school was across the street from his building. After circling the block Terry located a space and squeezed his tiny hatchback into it. He scuffed his boot heels up the inclined street and inspected the painted blue apartment house, tiny, three floors, with a set of steps to the white front door. On the panel by the key lock was a list of occupants' names. Whitehall was number 212. Trying the master key on his ring, the door opened and he climbed the stairs to the second floor. It smelled of dust and mold.

Standing in front of his apartment door, Terry used another key that resembled a house key and it opened his unit. He stepped inside, turning on lights as he went. It was tiny, one bedroom, with a bay window in the living room and no dining room.

TiMELESS

It was neatly kept and sparse. He immediately headed to the bedroom and looked at the rotary phone on his nightstand. Opening the drawer under it, he searched for an address book. Inside the drawer was a box of condoms, lubrication, a dildo, and issues of *Playgirl*. Distracted for a moment, he opened one magazine and unfolded the centerfold. Andrew Cooper III? *Wow*.

"Wait a minute. That's Sam Jones!" Terry recognized the star from an old 1980 Flash Gordon movie. Shaking his head, tossing the magazine back into the drawer, Terry went on the hunt for Paul's phone number. Once he had rummaged through the bedroom, he hunted inside kitchen drawers. Finally he located an address book.

Opening it up on the counter, he scanned the pages and read Paul Stevens' work and home number. Terry immediately reached for the wall telephone near the kitchen cabinets.

Using the rotary dial he wondered how the hell anyone could live without smart-phones, Skype, and mini-computers. It was maddening.

The phone connected and rang. He paced as far as the coiled cord would allow. No answering machine picked up, nor did Paul. "Come on! Where are you!" Terry began to panic. "No! No way!" He called the work phone number, even though it was well passed business hours. A recorded message picked up.

'*...thank you for calling Wellness Center. Our business hours are Monday through Friday eight to five pm. If you know the extension of your contact...*'

Terry hung up and rubbed his face as he walked to his living room. Sitting on a rust colored fabric sofa, he leaned his arm against the back, his chin on his arm, and stared at the swaying trees that grew on the verge in front of the apartment house. It was silent except for the wind rattling the wooden sash windows. "I didn't do it. I lost him again." He stared up at the ceiling and asked, "All I wanted was one day! How come I can't go back to the right one?"

Closing his eyes, Terry started to cry, knowing this experiment was futile, and even if he did arrive in the correct era, to the hour of his worst nightmare, how could he change history?

There was a bigger force working here than his own as well as the science that made what he did possible. But Terry couldn't give up. He had to at least try.

When the phone rang he leapt to his feet and sprinted to grab it. "Hello?"

"Is this Dan Whitehall?"

Terry's stomach pinched. "Yes. Oh God no."

"This is Detective Graves from the traffic unit of the Seattle Police Department."

"No! No!" Terry dug his hands through his hair.

"Do you know a young man named...Paul Stevens?"

Terry sank to the linoleum floor against the wall, the phone clenched in his hand as he failed yet again to prevent fate. "Yes. I know him."

"Your number was the only one we located for a contact. I wonder if you know Paul's family's information."

Though he already knew the answer, Terry asked, "What happened to Paul?"

"I'm afraid he was hit head on in an automobile collision."

"No..."

"He...he didn't make it. I'm sorry."

Terry released the phone and it spun, hitting against the wall as the cord unwound. He covered his face and cried.

TiMELESS

CHAPTER 7

We have to bring you home.
No! Don't! I haven't succeeded!
It's too dangerous. We can't control where you are!
You can't yet. Let me keep trying. Please!
Dr Lennox, it's not me that's making the decision.
No! It can't end yet! Please.

Terry fought to wake from a deep sleep. Noise of a radio or television news station became audible in his in-between state of slumber and consciousness.

'*...breaking news...we have just learned that President Saddam Hussein has just invaded Kuwait after accusing Kuwait of driving the price of oil down...*'

Terry opened his eyes instantly, lying horizontally on a sofa in a den.

'*...President Bush is going to make a statement soon to the public but our insiders state he will declare there is no justification whatsoever for this outrageous and brutal act of aggression...*'

Sitting up, rubbing his face, Terry knew immediately what year he had landed in. And the date. August, 1990.

He jumped out of his skin when someone entered the room with two cups of a steaming brew.

"You believe this?" the man said as he handed a mug to Terry and sat beside him. "That Saddam fucker is out of his mind if he thinks the world will put up with that."

Terry scooted over as this delicious man sat beside him, sipping his tea, focusing on the news. Terry sniffed the mug and it smelled like herbal green tea.

'*We will be cutting soon to the broadcast at the White House as the president prepares to address the nation...*'

Terry stared at this man's profile. Thirties? Stunning... conservatively cut brown hair, brown eyes, shirtless, a nice triangle of hair inverted in his chest, and a treasure trail to die for.

Knowing how the tale on the television ended, and began, and continued throughout decades to war in Afghanistan and throughout the Middle East, Terry placed his mug down on a side table and looked at his hands as if trying to assess his own age quickly without a mirror.

"You believe this?" the man gestured to the TV. When Terry didn't answer he said, "Sam? Where are you? Hello! The president is going to announce we're going to fucking war!"

"I'm Sam."

He got a strange look. "You okay?"

"Are we lovers?"

"Are you listening to what's going on in the news or what?"

"Shit. 1990. Fuck!"

"What the hell is wrong with you?" The gorgeous man gave Terry a weird look. "You must have really been out of it from your nap. You're delirious."

"Look at me."

He got an exhale of exasperation and a stare.

There he is. Sky. Why could Terry see him in every one of these men and Sky could not recognize him?

"How long have we been together?" Terry asked.

TiMELESS

"Not now. I want to see what the president is going to say."

Terry stood off the sofa and hunted for the bathroom. He located it and turned on a light, looking in the mirror. His jaw dropped. He touched his face and checked out his image, his bright blue eyes, his thick wavy brown hair that brushed his jaw line, and his rugby build. Taking his tank top off, he inspected his physique and then tugged down his gym shorts. "I have shitty luck fixing my life but damn, I'm doing good in the gorgeous-hunk category."

Tugging his shorts lower, he inspected his ass and spotted a small tattoo on his right ass cheek. He couldn't make it out. Opening the medicine cabinet he looked for anything with a hand mirror on it. But he wasn't likely to find a woman's compact in this place.

Asking himself, "Do we live together?" Terry pulled his shorts up and noticed two toothbrushes in the holder. "Yes? Do we?" He left the bathroom and spotted the bedroom right across the hall. "Where am I?" he mused quietly and found a wallet on the dresser. Looking back at the door, he picked it up and checked out the ID.

Jason W. McKenna, born in 1955, which makes my lover thirty-five, and we live in...San Francisco?

"Cool." He tugged out credit cards, thoroughly inspecting the contents of Jason's wallet, then set it down and tried to find his own. On his nightstand was another billfold. He opened it. *Sam B. Cavanaugh, born in 1960.* A five year age gap between them.

Terry removed an ID card from a college, seeing he was a professor at Berkeley. "Huh."

A noise behind him startled him. He put the wallet down and spun around.

"What's up, Sam?"

"Nothing, Jason." Terry admired his partner as Terry crossed the room. He caressed Jason's neck and ran his fingers down his chest to his belly button.

Jason's laugh was deep and masculine. "I take it you don't want to watch the news."

"I know how the story ends." Terry met Jason's eyes, begging him silently to see who he was.

"War. I know. But sometimes you have to fight."

"Is it the weekend?"

"Huh?" Jason caressed Terry's upper arms affectionately.

"I assume its Saturday or Sunday."

"What are you talking about? It's Wednesday night."

"Shit. Does that mean I have to work tomorrow?"

"You love that job." Jason backed Terry up against the bed and sat him down, running his hand over Terry's hair.

"Teaching at Berkeley. I hope it's a good subject." Terry stared at Jason's treasure trail and then down at the bulge in his shorts.

"You're a nut." Jason laughed and pushed Terry back on the bed, lying on top of him.

"Do you love me?" Terry caressed Jason's rough jaw.

"You know I do." Jason reached down to Terry's shorts and tugged at them. Terry raised his hips and Jason removed them, taking off his own as well. Once they were both nude, Terry bent his knees and spread his legs, allowing Jason between his thighs.

"Look at me." Terry caught Jason's chin in two fingers, before he went for his lips.

"What's gotten into you, Sam?"

"Baby. Please, look at me."

"My pleasure." Jason propped himself up and smiled, staring into Terry's eyes.

"Do you see me?"

"Oh yes. You should be a model, not a college prof."

"No, Sky…I mean, Jason. Look at me." Terry tried not to vent his frustration.

TiMELESS

Jason's smile dropped and he did, studying Terry carefully. "What am I looking for?"

"Your true love?" Terry's heart began to ache.

"You are my true love. Sam, what the hell's going on?"

Terry covered his face and moaned. "This is useless."

His arms were dragged down and pinned to the bed. "Tell me what's going on? I know this whole AIDS thing has the city reeling, and add to that now, this fucking war."

"Are we HIV positive, Jason?"

"No! Sam?" Jason went to sit up, move away.

Terry gripped him tightly. "Don't you dare get up."

"You're saying very odd things. How am I supposed to interpret them? Huh? Did you cheat? Should we get tested again?"

Terry didn't know if Sam cheated, but he said, "I would never cheat on you. Never."

"Then what's this all about? Are you still stressing about your parents?"

Terry perked up. "What did my parents do?"

"They won't talk to you. Ever since you came out."

"When did I come out?"

"Jesus!" Jason recoiled again as if he would stand up and leave the room.

"I'm thirty years old," Terry said, "Why would I care what my parents say now?"

"You do. You told me you're a mess that they keep ignoring you. The letters you write to your mom always come back unopened. Have you had a change of heart? Do you not care anymore?"

Terry embraced Jason and closed his eyes, pressing his face into Jason's neck. "Why do people behave that way about love?"

"You're the human sexuality professor, you tell me."

Terry's eyes blinked open. "I am?"

71

He felt Jason try to move back and held him tight so he couldn't. "I am," Terry said with more conviction. "My favorite subject." The news report was still airing in the background, but Terry tried to tune it out. He craved sex with Jason. Since losing Sky nothing mattered more to him than the closeness he and Sky shared.

"Make love to me." Terry held Jason's face in both hands.

Jason appeared to melt at the request and went for Terry's mouth. They kissed and Terry spread his legs wide in invitation.

Jason kissed Terry passionately, opening his mouth wider and swirling tongues, then he parted from Terry's lips and kissed his way to Terry's nipple.

Propping up his head on a pillow, Terry watched as Jason enjoyed him, chewing on one nipple, making it hard, and moving to the next. There was no doubt in Terry's mind that two gay men, living in San Francisco in the nineties, would know how to do everything to each other.

This wasn't 1960, and they weren't nineteen!

Jason licked his way down Terry's taut skin to his pubic hair, brushing against Terry's hard cock with his jaw and then lips.

Terry moaned and spread his arms wide across the downy bedding, staring up at the ceiling fan and remembering the first time he and Sky had made love. It was wild and out of control, two men who were so attracted to each other, they couldn't wait to be naked and grinding. And they had met on New Year's Eve.

He closed his eyes. It was so easy to envision it. Even the technique Jason was using was Sky's. Making light kisses along his length, Jason urged Terry to bend his knees tighter, and then went for Terry's rim.

"Know you love that." Terry laughed.

"Mm." Jason lapped at Terry's skin with wide, wet licks.

His balls were sucked and teethed playfully and Terry's cock became very interested in sex. He raised his head to see Jason's expression of lust and when Jason and he caught gazes, the sight of Sky in his eyes nearly made Terry choke in awe. Jason knelt up, grinning, rubbing his thumb over Terry's saliva-coated rim.

Terry looked back at the nightstand. "Rubbers and lube?"

"You know where they are."

With the assumption he did, Terry rolled to his side and opened the top drawer. He tore a condom off the strip and tossed it to Jason, then held the lubrication at the ready.

Jason rolled the condom on and held out his hand.

In anticipation, Terry shivered as he poured some onto Jason's fingers. Once Jason was prepared, he pushed his fingertips inside Terry and took the head of his cock into his mouth.

Terry let out a loud moan and tried to set the gel on the night table before he went into orbit.

While Jason drew his cock deep and fast, he worked Terry's hole like a pro. Like Sky.

"That's it." Terry bucked with the growing pleasure. He gripped the bedding and threw back his head. "How I have missed this. Oh, Christ."

His prostate getting a great heated friction rub, Terry's cock began to seep pre-cum and he was on the edge. Jason obviously tasted it and felt Terry's cock thicken to its potential because Jason thrust his hand faster, sucking deep strong suction.

Terry couldn't stop the climax if he tried. Deep pleasure swirls started in his balls and radiated to the tip of his dick and his ass. He parted his lips and couldn't believe the intensity or the memory of the incredible love he and his partner shared.

Just as the reverberations slowly subsided, Jason scooted closer, turned Terry slightly to his side, and pushed his cock in, hammering hard and deep.

Sweat running down Terry's temple, he watched Jason's chest and abs tighten as he thrust his hips, his face expressing his pleasure. Seeing Sky so clearly in Jason's handsome features, Terry was lost on how it could be possible that Sky's soul, or essence could in any way be inside another man.

Reincarnation? Terry didn't believe in it. Maybe he should.

"Oh yeah, oh, yeah!" Jason accelerated the action of his hips and Terry could feel his cock pulsate inside him.

When Jason grunted and came, Terry shivered and nearly became emotional. They were the same noises Sky made when he came. Identical.

A lover's fingerprint in Terry's opinion.

When Jason pulled out, catching his breath and staring at the condom, Terry dove at him, nearly knocking them off the foot of the bed.

Jason held on to prevent their fall and laughed as he stared at Terry. "I take it you enjoyed that."

"I love you, Sky!"

"Sky?" Jason's look of pleasure changed to suspicion.

"No. I mean, Jason. I'm just high from the climax."

Jason edged off the bed, out of Terry's grasp and didn't look convinced. "First you ask me if we're HIV positive, then you call me another guy's name?" He gave Terry a dirty look and left the room.

Terry scrambled off the bed and followed Jason to the bathroom, where he was removing the condom and washing up.

"I didn't cheat." Terry wet a washcloth and used it to clean up, trying to meet Jason's gaze in the mirror over the sink.

"Who's Sky?" Jason faced him, arms crossed.

"He's you."

Jason glared at him and left the bathroom.

When Terry caught up to Jason he was dressed in his gym shorts and sitting in front of the television, sipping the tea.

TiMELESS

Terry looked back at the news commentators getting a publicity-hard-on over the latest update of the growing tension in Iraq and Kuwait.

"Okay..." Terry sat on the wood flooring in front of Jason, touching his knee. "Listen to me."

"Not sure I want to even be in the same room as you at the moment."

Terry pointed to the television. "See that shit?"

Jason didn't respond, his cup to his lips, his vision glued to the television set.

"We get involved in this war, big time, in January," Terry tried to get Jason to pay attention. "There will be live coverage of raids, tracer missiles, the works, broadcasted on TV."

Jason gave Terry an odd glance and set his cup aside.

"We will liberate Kuwait in one month, after that. Then..."

Jason began paying attention to Terry but looked confused.

"We elect Bill Clinton in 1992, and he's re-elected in 1996."

"Who?"

"Bill Clinton the governor of Arkansas...never mind. Anyway," Terry tilted his head to get Jason to let it go so he could keep talking. "He gets impeached during his second term for letting a woman suck his cock but the impeachment is overturned and he serves out his term."

"Huh?" Jason didn't appear to be buying any of it.

"Fast forward to Bush junior being elected in 2001 and we get hit with a horrific terrorist attack on the Twin Towers in New York on September 11th ...two jet airplanes hit them making them collapse, and at the same time other planes are hijacked and—"

Jason held up his hand to stop him. "I have no idea what you're talking about but you're not making sense. The Twin Towers collapse? Come on." Jason gave him a look of disbelief.

Terry reached back and shut the television, sitting on the floor in front of Jason. "I tried this tactic before, but it didn't work."

"What tactic? Distracting me with bullshit so I don't believe you cheated on me with some guy named 'Sky'? Who names their kid Sky?" Before Terry replied, Jason asked, "Is he one of your students?"

"No. Look, Jason." Terry rested his elbows on Jason's knees to get closer to him. "My name is Terry Lennox."

Jason's eyes widened. "What the fuck? Have you been lying to me this whole time about who you are?" He appeared very confused. "Wait. You can't be someone else. The college does extensive background checks. What the hell is going on?"

"Will you let go of everything you believe and believe me?"

"I thought I did believe in you." Jason tried to push Terry off his lap.

Terry rubbed his face and looked at the blank TV screen, turning around and resting his back against the sofa. "I can't do this. I can't."

"Fine. Move out." Jason pointed the remote control at the set and turned it back on.

Terry looked at the ceiling and asked, mostly himself, "How am I supposed to get anyone to believe me? I wouldn't believe me."

"You're pissing me off."

Terry spun back around and leaned on the sofa beside Jason's legs. "You have no idea how frustrated I am right now."

"Just admit you cheated."

"No. I didn't cheat. I swear." He raised his hand in an oath. "But I am telling you the truth about everything." Terry looked at the television. "In the next couple of weeks there's going to be a disaster when the rigs are bombed and oil spills into the Persian Gulf. We're going to bomb the snot out of Iraq."

TiMELESS

Not hearing any rebuttal to his comment, Terry peeked over his shoulder. Jason was staring at him as if he had Martian antennas. "Okay, whatever." Terry shook his head. "Do you drink and drive?"

"What?" Jason looked at Terry in disbelief.

"Don't go anywhere tonight."

"I have a meeting at eight."

Terry panicked. "A meeting? Why?"

"Why?" Jason narrowed his eyes. "You just asked me if I drink and drive and now you want to know what the meeting is about?"

"AA?"

"I should get ready." Jason stood and walked to the bedroom.

"No!" Terry scrambled to run after him. "Don't go. You can't go!"

"Jesus, Sam." Jason shed the shorts and slipped on a pair of jeans. "You're really weird tonight. Go out for a run or something."

"I'm going with you." Terry opened a dresser drawer and tugged a shirt over his head.

"You're wearing my clothing?"

"Huh?" Terry looked down at the top. "No?"

"Whatever." Jason opened the closet and took a short-sleeved shirt off a hanger.

"Where do I keep my jeans?" Terry asked, knowing he'd get a strange reaction.

Jason threw a pair at him and they landed on Terry's head.

Sighing, Terry dragged them off and stepped into them, zipping them up and tucking in the shirt.

"I'm not cool with you coming. You never come to my meetings and you shouldn't."

"I'll wait in the car." Terry stuffed his wallet into his pocket and looked for a mobile phone. When he noticed a big bulky one sitting in a charger he picked it up. It was warm to his touch. It had a retractable plastic antenna and felt enormous compared to his personal electronic device. "We've come a long way, baby."

"Huh?"

"Nothing." Terry noticed a boxy white computer in the corner on a desk with a white matching keyboard. "Seriously."

Jason ignored him and reached out his hand. "That's my phone."

Terry gave it to him. "Do I have one?"

"You're too cheap to buy one." He walked out of the room. "I still don't know why you're coming with me. You said you had a ton of work to do for your lecture tomorrow."

"There won't be a tomorrow for me." Terry checked around the room, just noticing the details, while Jason shut off the television and lights; framed posters of Madonna and Bette Midler were on the walls.

"What the hell is that supposed to mean?" Jason stopped short before he left the apartment.

Terry stood nose to nose with his man. "If you don't believe me, I most likely can't prevent what's going to happen. And it will kill me over and over again." Terry choked up.

"Baby?" Jason held Terry's arms and tried to look him in the eye. "Nothing will happen. You worry too much."

"Where's the AA meeting?" Terry dabbed at his eyes as they filled.

"You know where it is. They had to move it since the quake." Jason held his keys and left the apartment, walking down the stairs to the ground floor.

"Quake!" Terry shut the door and hurried after him. "Of course! The earthquake of 1989!"

Jason gave him another queer glance as he left their home and walked towards the street. He stood at the driver's side door of a red 1990 Mazda Miata.

TiMELESS

"Love these things." Terry admired the pretty little roadster. "How much is gas?"

"A friggin rip-off. Last I filled it up it was a buck nineteen."

"Damn. Beats five dollars a gallon. Thank fuck we're finally off fossil fuels." Terry sat in the bucket seat and fastened his belt. When Jason didn't right away, Terry reached out to do it for him.

"Hey. I'll do it myself. Why are you so uptight? I swear, Sam, if you embarrass me tonight…"

"No. I won't. I'll sit in the car." Terry touched the dash. "No passenger airbag?"

"Will you chill?" Jason shook his head in annoyance.

Terry slouched low in the seat, hoping now that he was with Jason, he had accomplished something. But what would remain to be seen.

CHAPTER 8

While the car stereo played Seal's *Crazy*, Terry looked around the neighborhoods as they rode by. Since it was August it was mild and overcast, with long days and short nights. Summer in San Francisco, not boiling August sun, more like soggy foggy cold damp days. After a twenty minute drive, where Terry was watching every oncoming car with dread and apprehension, Jason parked in a parking lot of a school.

He shut off the engine and stared at Terry, holding out the key. "I can't believe you want to sit in the car."

"I can come in."

"No." Jason exited the vehicle and vanished inside the building.

Terry slouched in the seat, pulling it back so he could stretch out his legs, even reclining it so he could rest. He stared at the plastic ceiling and dome light as other cars pulled in around him, most likely not noticing he was even there, since he was below the window line.

He put the key into the ignition and kept the radio on. Music of the 90's...Nirvana, Radiohead...a time capsule of a generation.

The world wasn't so different from day to day, but the culture? The political climate? Each decade brought huge upheaval and change. Wars, natural disasters, medical breakthroughs and more disease resistant viruses...

TiMELESS

Terry closed his eyes as the music changed to a soft melody, *Tears in Heaven*, Eric Clapton.

We're bringing you back, Dr Lennox. We have to while we can.
No! Just give me another few hours! I can't go back now. I'm there! Don't you get it? I can do it.
There's something urgent we need to tell you. Please listen carefully. The data we entered into the code has been hacked. We...unfortunate...locked on...no way to...misdirected—

Terry opened his eyes and smelled burning rubber and plastic. Red and blue lights were spinning around him and a deep blast from a fire truck's air horn made him jump out of his skin.

"Let's go!"

Terry felt a slap on his back and it hit with a strange thud. He looked down at himself and he was wearing a San Francisco police uniform. He took one step and could see a wreckage in front of him, two cars, hit head on.

One was a 1990 red Mazda Miata, the other? A large diesel truck with a container on its trailer.

Terry couldn't think straight and hurried over to the crash as firemen and cops flooded the scene, diverting traffic and treating the injured.

He looked inside the Miata and one man, bleeding from his forehead was being stabilized by a fireman who was holding his neck. The man was crying and calling out the name, "Jason!"

Terry's stomach pinched and he made his way to the driver's side of the car to see the firefighters using the Jaws-of-Life to open the small car. Inside, behind the wheel, the driver was slumped over, not moving.

"West!" An officer with sergeant stripes on his shoulder addressed him. "Stop gawking and get that intersection blocked! Where's your high-visibility vest!"

Terry was slow to react, hearing Eric Clapton's *Tears in Heaven* playing from the damaged car's radio along with the sobs of the man in the passenger's seat, while the lifeless body of the driver was being removed to a gurney.

"No!" Terry yelled. "No! I stopped this from happening!"

Another cop shoved an orange vest with the word POLICE written on the back at Terry. "Let's go, West! I need help here!"

Terry took the vest, trying to put it on and cried, "What happened? I was there to prevent this! No!"

His arm was grabbed and one of his fellow officers dragged him to a patrol car which was running, hot to the touch, and had all its lights flashing. "Pull yourself together! What the fuck has gotten into you, Tom?"

The cop helped Terry put the traffic vest over his uniform. The weight of Terry's gun belt and bullet proof vest suddenly felt like lead around his body.

"West!"

When Terry could not move or function, the second officer shook him to get him to focus. "What the hell is going on? Light some flares and help me out!"

Terry was shoved to the back of a patrol car and the trunk opened. A handful of road flares were given to him and he was pushed to get moving.

Holding the red waxy sticks, Terry watched the driver of the Miata being given CPR, but he knew. Jason McKenna was already dead. Sam Cavanaugh? Crying, screaming in agony at the loss of his lover, as he too was strapped to a gurney and wheeled to an ambulance.

TiMELESS

The traffic was nightmarish as the emergency responders clogged the intersection. Tears ran down Terry's cheeks while he lit the flares and had no idea where or how to place them. He walked against the flow of gawkers, waving the flaming end at them to get them to move away, then began dropping them as he went, until he had walked an entire block and lit the last flare. He looked back at the chaotic scene and fell apart.

"I was there!" he screamed, staring at the night sky. "I was fucking there!" he yelled at the top of his lungs.

Noise of a shoe scuffing the pavement as it ran towards him made Terry turn around. A hand grabbed his arm and he was dragged to patrol car and forced to sit down sideways on the passenger's seat. The young cop who had given him the flares crouched beside him. "What's going on, Tom?"

"I prevented this!" Terry used his uniform sleeve cuff to wipe his eyes.

"How could you have? Huh? We were handling a fucking DV call five miles away?"

Terry hid his face and crouched over his lap.

"I have never seen you fall apart, man. You're freaking me out."

Terry shook his head, not looking at the officer, and curled up in a ball over his lap. He heard voices near him.

"I have no idea, Sarge. He's cracking up on me. I can't babysit him right now."

"Go. I'll take care of it."

Terry felt a hand on his shoulder. "Tom? Come with me."

"Where?" Terry tried to see through his tears.

"Come on." The sergeant coaxed him out of the patrol car and walked Terry to another one nearby. He was again nudged to sit down, the door shut for him, and then the sergeant walked around to the driver's side and got behind the wheel. Another officer in a uniform with chevron stripes on his sleeve stood by the sergeant seated beside Terry. Terry heard one say to the other, "He's having a breakdown. I'm bringing him back to the station."

"Okay. I got it covered. The traffic unit has showed up so your boys will be clearing the scene soon."

"Okay."

Terry closed his eyes and felt hot tears run down his face.

The car moved slowly at first, then picked up speed.

Leaning his elbow against the armrest, Terry hid his face and had no idea how he could have failed. He was there!

The police radio crackled with broadcasts but Terry not only couldn't decipher them, he didn't care.

It was code. Strange sounding secret code.

Like a foreign language.

He looked down at his hands. They were sooty from the flares and felt coated with the wax. His uniform pants were dirty from them. The orange vest was open and hanging off his shoulders. A gun was on his right hip and his belt was overloaded with gear; handcuffs, flashlight, expandable baton, mace, magazines for bullets...it was absurd how much weight he was hauling, like a mule, and that didn't count for the heavy Kevlar vest.

The sergeant pulled into the back of a police station, parking and shutting the car. Before he opened the door, he looked at Terry. "Tom."

Terry forced himself to look at him.

"What's going on? You've been on the force for nearly twenty years."

"I don't know how I could have fucked up."

The sergeant tilted his head. "Are we talking about the accident? Or did you do something you want to tell me about?"

"That man shouldn't have died. Jason McKenna."

"Did you know him?"

"Yes." Terry's lip quivered.

TIMELESS

"How did you know that man?" When Terry didn't answer the sergeant asked, "Tom? Was he a friend of yours?"

What was Terry supposed to say? It was then he looked down at his left hand. There was a gold band on his ring finger. He pulled the visor down and gazed into the mirror behind it. A man in his forties, graying temples, piercing blue eyes, was staring back.

"Oh no." Terry suddenly had a feeling this time the leap went horribly wrong. "Am I...straight?"

The sergeant coughed uncomfortably. "Tom, you've been married for nearly twenty years. Do I need to take you to the hospital for an eval?"

"No." Terry shook his head and climbed out of the car, trying to get a grip on himself.

The sergeant walked around the car to him. "Look, its nearing shift change. Go home."

In hopes of gaining sanity or at least some kind of calm, Terry investigated the area around him; it was filled with patrol cars and in the distance was a line of personal vehicles along the back fence. The police precinct was well lit and modern, for a 1990's era building.

"Home." Terry's eyes burned. *I've no idea where that is anymore.*

"Come on. Go get changed out of your gear and go home."

The sergeant walked with Terry to the back entrance, using a code in a security box to gain access. Inside the police station was a maze of rooms, write up areas with cops at computers, desks with more men with rank; chevrons on their sleeves or gold bars on the collars, writing or talking on the phone. Overhead florescent bulbs lit the walls of long corridors which were covered with corkboards plastered with wanted posters, suspect warning information and pages of rules and regulations.

"Where am I going?" Tom asked.

His sergeant appeared even more upset. "You don't know the way to the locker room?"

"No." Terry could see this man was assuming he was either crazy or having a nervous breakdown.

"I'm starting to wonder if you've had a stroke." The sergeant's concern grew. "Do I need to get you to the ER?"

"No. I'm just overwhelmed. I can't think straight."

He was escorted to the locker room and even his locker was pointed out. Terry had no idea the combination but he nodded in thanks and the sergeant left. Terry took his wallet out of his back trouser pocket and began to investigate the contents. Thomas E. West, born 1947, which if this was still 1990 made him forty-three. He found photos which he assumed were his wife and kid. Also, a tiny scrap paper with a combination on it. He tried the numbers on his locker and it opened.

Inside were civilian clothes. He changed, hanging up his gun belt and uniform on the hooks and put on a pair of baggy slacks and button down shirt. Once he was dressed he noticed a set of keys on the top shelf of the locker and inspected it. A car or truck key with an alarm fob on it was clustered with a number of other generic keys.

Terry closed the locker door and without acknowledging the uniformed men coming and going in the locker room, he left the way he had come in. Next he wandered the parking lot, holding out the fob and pressing it to see which car reacted.

A pickup truck made a chirping noise and its lights flashed. He sat behind the wheel and again took a look at his driver's license to see the address. Though he was a San Francisco cop, he lived in Walnut Creek. After searching the glove box for a map without success, Terry drooped in the bench seat and rested his head on the headrest.

TiMELESS

"I was there. I was sitting in that car waiting for Jason to come out of the AA meeting. How could I have not stayed long enough to stop that accident? I don't understand. And..." He looked down at himself. "Why am I still in 1990 in some straight married guy's body? I swear I am so fucking lost."

He closed his eyes and had no idea what to do or where to go.

A tapping at the glass near him startled him. Terry jolted and spotted a woman, close to his own age, standing beside his truck. Terry started the engine and powered the window down.

"Tom! Your sergeant called me. He said I should come down right away."

Terry recognized her from a picture in his wallet and assumed it was his wife. "I don't feel well."

She reached in and touched his forehead. "Come home."

"Can I follow you?"

"I'm parked right out there." She pointed beyond the enclosed perimeter of the station's fence. "Are you okay to drive?"

"Yes." He sat up and tried to appear normal, which was absurd.

She nodded and hurried away. Terry immediately drove behind her as she walked, having no other easy way to find where he lived.

The woman entered a mid-sized sedan, older than 1990, and Terry stuck to her bumper like a dog sniffing another dog's back end, in order to not lose her. After a half hour drive, one in which he was preoccupied so deeply he couldn't have recalled the name of any street he drove down, the car he followed slowed. She pulled into a driveway of an up-scale home, two stories, split-level, with a two car garage. Terry parked his pickup beside her car and stepped out of the truck, following her to the inner door, which connected to the kitchen. It was open-plan and clean, clutter free with the scent of cooking permeating the home. Once inside the home, Terry heard music coming from the upper floor. Loud, grunge-era rock.

"Dinner is warming in the oven." She put her purse and keys on the counter. "Do you feel well enough to eat?"

"I'm fine. Let me wash my hands." Terry followed the source of the music and came to a closed door on the second floor. He knocked but no doubt the music was so loud it couldn't be heard. Terry opened the door.

A young man, possibly mid to late teens, jumped out of his skin at his entry. He was lying on the floor, a magazine near him, talking on the phone. "I'll call you back." The young man hung up. The fear in his eyes confused Terry.

"Dad! Uh...You're home early." The young man kicked the magazine under his bed and sat up, running his hand through his shaggy hair and looking so terrified Terry wondered if the man he occupied had issues with his son.

"Can you lower that?" Terry pointed to the music system.

His request was jumped to, as if it were an order. The young man stood shaking like a leaf after he shut off the music.

"Am I that scary?" Terry asked.

The look on the young man's face was stunned.

"Am I?" Terry stepped closer and the young man nearly fell over himself backing up.

"Tom! Tyler! Dinner is on the table!" was called from below.

"Tyler." Terry now knew the young man's name. "What the hell did I do to you to make you react like a kicked puppy?"

"Huh?" Tyler's eyes widened. "Are you kidding me?...uh, Sir."

"Sir?" Terry rubbed his face and felt the wax still on his hands. "Jesus. I'm a fucking monster." He walked out of the room and located a master bedroom containing large, dark wood furniture, perfectly kept, and not a speck of dust. He turned on the light in the adjoining bathroom and washed his hands and face, staring at himself in the mirror. He didn't look too horrible. Just slightly worn out, getting gray at the temples, and not cut or muscular, but not heavy either. He dried his hands and leaned on the sink to stare into his blue eyes. "What did you do to your son? Hm, ya bastard?"

Terry may not have been able to help Jason, but he was going to do something this time. He left the bathroom and spotted Tyler still in his bedroom, trying to straighten it up, like if he didn't, he'd be grounded, or worse.

Terry stopped at the door. "Tyler. Are you hungry?"

"I'm sorry the room's a mess. I'll clean it up."

In disbelief Terry stepped in, Tyler flinched and backed up.

"Do I hit you? What the hell?"

Tyler shivered and gave Terry a look that answered his own question. "Do I? I do? Why do I hit you?"

"Huh?" Tyler bit his lip. "Because I'm a loser fag who won't amount to anything?"

"I call you that?" Terry felt sick to his stomach.

"Tom? Are you coming down? Dinner is on the table!"

"One minute!" Terry yelled and then pointed to the bed. "Sit."

Obeying, again as if it were an order, Tyler sat, hunched over, not meeting Terry's eye.

Terry took his place beside the young man and rubbed his eyes tiredly. "I'm a bastard if I say things like that to you."

Tyler didn't respond, as if he didn't dare.

"How old are you?"

"Fourteen, sir."

"Stop saying sir."

"Yes, sir...I mean... yes."

"Does your mother know I hit you?" Terry felt so much sympathy for this young boy he was about to beat up the body he inhabited to give it a taste of its own medicine.

Tyler shrugged as if he didn't know, or wouldn't answer.

"Hand me that pad and pen on your desk."

Tyler did.

Terry turned to a fresh page and wrote, '*I, Tom West, Tyler's dad, love him without condition and will turn myself into the authorities if I ever lay a finger on him again. I promise to respect his choices, allow him to be the man he is, support him in his decisions and be there for him if he succeeds or fails. This is my word of honor.*' And he signed it. He tore the sheet out of the pad and handed it to Tyler. "Hold onto this. If I hit you again, call the cops."

Tyler gave him a sarcastic glare then his expression straightened.

"Oh. Right. I'm a cop. Okay, call child protective services. You have one of those in this town?"

"I guess so."

"Tom! Dinner is getting cold!"

"Your mother wants us to eat dinner while its hot." Terry put his arm around Tyler and felt him tense up in either fear or revulsion. "I love you. A father is supposed to love his kids. No if's ands or buts. And I want you to make sure the next time I get out of hand...and I mean it!" He shook Tyler. "You get me the help I need."

"You okay?" Tyler looked into Terry's eyes. And for just a brief second, Terry felt as if Tyler saw something other than his bastard dad in them.

"No. Obviously I've got issues and I need years of meds and therapy, but I doubt I'll ever get it. Just listen to me now. Don't stop being who you want to be. In a few years you'll be independent and can do what you want. You got that?"

"You won't let me go to Berkeley. You said it's a lefty hippie college."

"Give me the paper back." Terry added to the note saying out loud as he wrote, "And my son can go to the college of his choice with our financial help." He looked at Tyler. "Can we afford to send you?"

Tyler laughed and then nodded.

"Good." He added to the note, "And I will never cut you out of the will."

"Wow. Dad. What happened to you? You're like a totally different guy."

"Yeah. Thank fuck, right?" Terry gave Tyler the note. "Show that to your mother now. I want to make sure she's on board."

"Mom's okay." He shrugged, looking down at the paper.

"Is she a good cook?" Terry stood and gestured for Tyler to go first.

"Yeah. She is." He laughed and shook his head. "That's one thing you never complain about."

Terry followed the young man down the stairs. "Yeah, I'm one fucked up bastard, aren't I?"

Tyler whipped his head around and blinked. "You said that, not me."

Terry laughed and knew it must be pretty bad to live with someone like that.

"Well! You two took your time!"

"Show your mother my note." He sat down at the head of the table.

"What's this?" the woman asked as she took the paper and Tyler sat down to eat.

Terry gave her time to read it. "Mm. It is good. Thanks for making a nice dinner, uh…sweetheart." He had no idea her name.

"You wrote this?" She held the page out to Terry in disbelief.

"Yeah," Terry said between bites of the chicken fillet. "If I give him a hard time…and I mean for anything!" He pointed his fork at her, "Kick my ass, will you? For crying out loud! I hit him and you know about it? And you let me?"

Her hand shook and she appeared pale.

"Do I hit you too?" Terry gasped.

"No! Tom, no. You never hit me."

"Mom, sit down. You look like you're about to faint."

She did, rereading the note.

"Look," Terry said, "I don't care if he's straight, bi, gay or wants a sex change. You got that...uh, dear?"

"What happened to you tonight?" She put the page aside and picked up her fork but didn't eat. "Your sergeant said you were on the scene of a fatality accident and you really got shook up."

"Yeah. I did. Life's too short. And I'm an ass." Terry heard Tyler laugh.

"If I go back to my 'old self'", Terry pointed at his wife, "It's up to you to fix it. You got it? Call the damn child services, get my ass thrown in jail. Maybe getting fucked behind bars will do me good."

Tyler choked with laugher and the woman at the table just choked.

Terry met her eyes. "I mean it. No matter what kind of fucking bastard I turn into. You keep several copies of that because I'm likely to rip it up and say I never wrote it." Terry sipped the glass of liquid and coughed when he realized it was a potent rum and coke. "Shit! I drink this at dinner?"

Tyler doubled over with laughter and said, "Man, what have you done with my dad? I actually like you."

"I like you too, kid." Terry winked at him and said to the astonished woman beside him. "Are you on Tyler's side or not?"

"Yes. I am," she said.

"Good. Then he goes to Berkeley and does whatever he wants. He said we can afford it." Terry sniffed the booze and shook his head. "That is so strong I'd be looped on half of it."

"Tom? What happened at work today?" She finally began eating.

"Seeing someone I love die. Believe me. It's hard as hell."

"Who died?" She panicked.

"Jason McKenna."

"I don't know him. Do I? Was he an officer you work with?"

"No. He's a gay guy I loved once."

Tyler choked on his food for real this time and began coughing.

"You need the Heimlich?"

"I'm good." Tyler held up his hand. "Dad?"

"Yeah?"

"I'm gay."

Terry looked at his wife as if he expected her to react and she was looking at him the same way. "Cool." Terry smiled. "You cool with that, wife?"

"Yes! I was afraid you would either kill him or he'd be so upset at your reaction he'd kill himself."

Terry put his fork down and met Tyler's gaze. "You were thinking of killing yourself?"

Tyler grew shy and didn't meet his eyes.

"Fuck!" Terry slammed his fist on the table making them both jump. "How can a father drive his son to this? Huh? Well, if I do anything to you, you take my gun and shoot me! You got it?" Terry pushed his plate away in fury. "Son of a bitch. I hate men like that."

"My word, Tom! You really went through something life altering tonight. I don't even recognize you anymore."

"Good." Terry picked up his drink and considered another sip, then said, "Oh! Shit. Is knowing I had a gay lover going to mess you up? uh…dear?"

"How long ago was it?" she asked.

"How long have we been married?"

Tyler cracked up again.

"Twenty years." The woman raised an eyebrow at him.

He waved her off. "Way before that. Hey, do we still have sex?"

Tyler went beet red and giggled.

"No. Not lately."

"We will tonight." Terry nodded. "I'll get it up for you. I promise."

"Too much info, Dad!" Tyler smiled.

He looked at his wife and son, savored their bright smiles and happy expressions and hoped to hell once he was gone, Tom West would not fuck up the repairs he had made. But once Terry vanished, he had no way of doing a Goddamn thing.

He gave his woman a smile and said, "We good, wife?"

"We're good, hubby." She reached out her hand.

Terry clasped it. "Being straight is too easy." He looked at Tyler. "You won't be able to marry a guy for a long time to come. Sucks."

"Yeah, Dad. It sucks." Tyler met his eyes and it made Terry shiver, as if Tyler knew exactly who he was.

Terry gave him a wink and Tyler winked back.

TiMELESS

CHAPTER 9

Terry opened his eyes.

The most incredible man he had ever seen in his life was lying crossways in the front seat of a car, naked from the waist up, wearing tight black pants and high glossed leather shoes. Under his trousers was a large bulge, ridiculously big. Terry thought of the gay porn stars he admired in 3-D plasma-real-TVD movies he and Sky had dual-loaded on their visor scanners.

"Are you going to stare or take the bloody picture?"

"Huh?" Terry realized he was holding a digital camera and leaning into the car.

"Bleedin' hell, mate! I'm not happy about this! Not one bit!"

A hand touched Terry from behind. "Armand, let me talk to Mr Richfield."

Terry backed up as a gray-haired older man wearing a suit, leaned into the sexy luxury sports car and said, "The sooner you get through this, the better."

"Drew, honestly. A flamin' dildo in my trousers? That's tack! I have no idea why you think you need to do this to sell bloody cars!"

Terry blinked at the comment and looked around. He was standing in an enormous studio which held three high end automobiles shined to a mirror's gleam. He was surrounded by lights and backdrops, assistants were everywhere, as well as a small group of staunch older men wearing business suits, observing, arms crossed, appearing pinched.

"Mark, we want you and our product to be the most controversial billboard on Santa Monica Boulevard. Humor us."

Terry looked at the camera in his hands, scrolling back through what appeared to be a very provocative photo shoot of a man named Mark Richfield. Judging by the cars and the technology, Terry estimated the year to be 2012? 2013?

"Humor you!" the stunner in the car with the long luxurious mane of hair removed a large dildo from his trousers making Terry gape in awe. "You know where you can bloody stick this?" Mark Richfield appeared about to rip the older man's head off.

The older man, whom Mark had called 'Drew' grabbed Terry's arm and shoved him back to the car again. "He's under contract, Armand, you get him to look sexy or else."

"Wow." Terry watched the older man in a suit storm away. "What on earth am I doing here?" Terry shook his head and approached the sports car timidly as a pretty, young African American woman powdered the model's face in the interim.

Terry waited until she backed out of the car, rolling her eyes at Terry as if she too thought the dildo idea was pretty outrageous. Holding his camera, Terry knelt into the car again as Mark shoved the phallus into his ridiculously tight pants once more.

"I'm sorry," Terry said, "I have nothing to do with these decisions."

"I'm not taking it out on you...but." Mark gestured to the bulge. "It's humiliating!"

"Christ, you are so fucking beautiful. How did you vanish from history? I have to look you up."

"What?" Mark tilted his head. "Did you say I vanished? Where the bloody hell did I go?"

TiMELESS

"Nothing." Terry looked down at the bulge. "Can you make it at least look real? It's not very convincing."

"Bloody hell!" Mark roared.

"Fine! Fine." Terry held the camera up as Mark reluctantly shifted the large dildo to at least appear slightly realistic in its angle. Looking at the display on his camera, Terry shook his head. "Man oh man. You are something else, mister."

"Thank you. Just take the bloody pictures. I'm already late."

Terry began taking shots of this unbelievable beauty, pout and all. "Um. Can you even try to smile? Or look like your sultry self? The frown is really a downer."

"Sod off."

"Mark," Terry leaned closer as he spoke, "Sex sells. Okay? And you? In this fucking orgasm machine is already giving me a boner. I don't need you to have that bulge but...uh...to be honest? Young men and women will be doing themselves to this ad for years. Believe me."

A slight upturned curl to this beauty's mouth appeared. "Take the bloody picture." His expression softened and Terry's skin burned from his sex appeal. The guy even smelled good.

"Better." Terry held up the camera and took shot after shot, every angle, loving the sensuous glares Mark was giving him staying hard the entire time he photographed this stud.

He stepped back from the car and scanned through his digital images. He had nearly a hundred. The dildo was tossed out of the passenger's door and bounced near Terry's feet. Mark exited the driver's side, running his hands back through his hair and appearing exhausted.

Terry looked back at Drew. "Anything else?"

"Let me look." Drew waved Terry closer, and Terry gave him the camera, staring at Mark as he crossed his arms over his hairless chest and waited impatiently. *Who are you? How has your image*

been erased from the world? Damn. You are the most unbelievable
male model I have ever seen.

"Good work, Armand. I know how hard it must be to work with
a prima dona like Mark." Drew gave him his camera back.

"I don't know if he's a prima dona, but he's worth every penny
you're paying him."

Drew made a noise in his throat of annoyance and he and his
cronies left the studio.

"I guess we're done, Mr Richfield." Terry walked closer to
Mark.

"Do. Not. Call me that!" Mark appeared at his wit's end.

"What should I call you?"

"Mark!"

Terry held up his hands in defense at the tone.

"Oh, love, I am so sorry." Mark lowered his voice and shook his
head. "I'm a mess about this shoot. Please forgive me. No need to
take it out on you. No need."

"Hey. I get it. You…uh…you have time for a drink?"

"No, my pet. I must get home. I'm already late." Mark began
walking to a man who had a rolling portable rack with clothing
hanging on from it.

Terry followed Mark like a puppy. "Um. Are you dating
anyone?"

As he put a shirt on, Mark turned around and appeared surprised.
"I'm married, Armand. I thought everyone in the world knew about
me and Steven."

"I must have forgotten. Your beauty made me stupid." Terry
smiled. "So, legal same sex marriage. Finally?"

"Huh?" Mark put his jacket on. "Where? Not here in California?
Oh no, love, they overturned it."

"What? Oh no. Come on!" Terry held the camera tight to his
chest and felt sick.

"Yes, well, a small leap forward, and two back. Such is the way. 'Night, love."

Terry watched him leave, staring at his ass as he went. The wardrobe assistant nudged him, waking him out of his stupor.

"Fucker's hot, isn't he? Damn."

"Yes. I'll say. I'm surprised his image wasn't carried forward through the decades. He's exceptional."

"Huh?"

"Never mind." Terry shook his head and asked, "Where am I supposed to go now?"

"Home?"

"Good." Terry noticed a carrying case for his camera, which included various lenses, and packed it away. He patted his pocket and when he felt a mobile device he looked up at the suspension ceiling and whispered, *'Thank you.'*

As he made his way to the exit, he scrolled through the applications on his phone and was so grateful for the information he nearly did a happy dance. Outside the studio was a large parking lot. Since it was just getting dark out, Terry figured it was either fall or the beginning of spring. He checked his phone for the date and time. Eight-forty-five, September 16th, 2012. California license plates were on every car, and he knew the area enough to know he was in So-Cal. And judging by the skyline? LA.

'Home' geographically, but on the time continuum? Not there yet. He used his car key fob to hunt down his vehicle. A snazzy black Pontiac Solstice gave him a sexy flash of its lights.

"Hmm. I do well. This looks promising." He sat down behind the wheel of his cozy coop and scanned through his phone messages. He had a text from someone named Clay Burrows that read, *'Luv u, cum home!'*

With technology finally on his side, Terry took a moment to assess everything. His driver's license read Armand Legrand, and he was very good looking, even in the crappy photo on the ID, he was thirty, and lived in Bel Air. The young man texting him was a mere twenty-one, and judging by the pictures of them together on his phone, stunning! He looked up the directions to his address, smiling at actually having a guidance system to get him there, then did research on everything he could think of, including himself.

He was a professional freelance photographer who had a spectacular website, photographed mostly men in various stages of undress, as well as porn stars. The amount of hits on the search engines was impressive. He opened his social network account, since the phone knew his passwords and he viewed his network of friends, and even his family. He had two younger sisters who seemed to like him, since they posted daily on his wall, and even his mother and father had profiles, and they too appeared supportive. Rainbow groups of all types were represented on his 'likes' pages and Terry hoped at least his only goal was to change one event, not fight with bastards who were ignorant, right? After all, this was 2012 and no one was anti-gay anymore, were they?

Terry tried to think back in history since he was born in 2035 so he had no clue other than to sit down tonight and research the world of politics to determine what was what when it came to the gay timetables of society. As far as history, politics, geography? He knew it all, but as far as when it was okay to just be gay...that he wasn't sure of.

But his main goal was to get to Clay and keep him safe.

He started the car and allowed the navigation system to direct him home.

In thirty minutes he was driving down a wide avenue lined with large multimillion dollar mansions, headed towards one in particular. He pulled into the driveway and elevated the garage door with the remote on his visor. The technology was better, but still so far behind where he was in his life in the future.

TiMELESS

Seeing gasoline at nearly four dollar a gallon, Terry was glad by the time he was in his thirties, fossil fuels were on their way out, replaced by clean alternatives. The end of the oil era for mankind. It was a good place to be in the timeline of humanity as far as the environment and human rights but the world had gone through hell to achieve it.

He took his gear out of the car to see a young man eagerly awaiting his arrival at the door connecting the garage to the house. Terry smiled at him. "Hello, Clay."

"Let me see! Let me see!" Clay waved to the camera eagerly. "I want to be there when you download them! Oh my God! Mark Antonious Richfield. Could ya die?"

Terry cupped Clay's face asking himself, 'could *you* die?'

Clay grabbed Terry's free hand and dragged him into the house, through an enormous open-space with minimalist décor; a white sectional sofa, bright colored accents, bronze male nudes on pedestals, and quite possibly Armand's own photographs of nubile young men were exhibited on every wall. As he passed the kitchen area there were windows overlooking a pool and hot tub. He continued on until Clay nudged him into a room, which appeared to be a home office with an enormous flat-screen computer monitor and stacks of camera equipment and hard drives.

As if Clay may be a model himself, his image was framed and on the wall, sultry, ridiculously young. Twenty-one?

"Where's the camera? Let me help you upload." Clay held out his hand.

Terry handed it to him, kissing his cheek.

"Mm." Clay smiled in delight and leaned against Terry for a nice tongue kiss.

"Uh, while you do that, let me wash up." Terry caressed Clay's soft blond hair. He stared deeply into Clay's blue eyes for a sign of

Sky but struggled this time. Blue eyes. Wrong color. Did that matter?

"Okay." Clay sat down at the computer desk and began plugging the camera into the hard drive.

Terry located a bathroom and looked at his reflection. He was a nice looking fellow, much like his driver's license photo, with dark black hair and his own blue eyes. Terry touched the designer stubble on his jaw and checked out his expensive clothing; a light cotton crew neck top and dark slacks. He raised the shirt up to see several tattoos, knowing they were all the rage in the decade he had landed in. He spun around to see his back and had a few there as well. Wriggling his pants down his legs, he was shaven, devoid of a pubic bush and had a decent cock, not too large, or too small. Nicely proportioned. His chest had been waxed and he felt some nubs on it.

A thirty year old man certainly wouldn't be smooth everywhere, but again Armand became a product of his era. Just like 1960 when he dated a man with greased back hair like Elvis.

He washed up, relieved himself and stepped out of the bathroom to see Clay, ogling the model's pictures.

Clay met Terry's gaze and moaned. "You lucky shit. Is that his real dick?"

"No. They made him stick a dildo into his pants." Terry scooted closer on a chair with wheels, looking at the pictures as they downloaded.

"Well, it's that big. You remember the nude pic he did in that UK gay mag issue."

"Uh...sure." Terry hadn't a clue. "Look, Clay, you don't drink and drive, do you?"

"Huh?" Clay gave Terry a strange look and then his focus went back to ogling. "That one! Look at his green eyes! Oh, babe, print that one just for me."

102

TiMELESS

"Should I be jealous?" Terry laughed and dug his fingers into the back of Clay's blond hair.

"Never." Clay kissed him and when Terry opened his eyes, he could see Clay watching the pictures still downloading. It made him laugh.

"Right," Terry said, "Do we eat dinner this late? Or am I the only one hungry?"

"We can go out. It's not that late. It's only nine."

"Out? No." Terry knew if they were in a car, on the road…well, the end result would be the same. "No. I'll order food in."

"Order in?" Clay blinked at him. "You never do that. We usually hit WeHo for a bite and dance after." Clay's attention was back on the screen. "Can that man take a bad picture? Hawt!"

Terry leaned over Clay's shoulder to see Mark's sultry glare in each photograph. They scanned though images where the model was leaning against a car front fender or grill, and of course the controversial ones inside as he sprawled over the front seat. "Is he known for his bad attitude?"

"Who? Mark?" Clay pointed at the computer. "Nope. Sweet as sugar. Him and his son."

"Son? He's straight?"

Clay stopped gawking at the photos and stared at Terry oddly. "What are you talking about?"

"Nothing." Terry took out his mobile phone and searched the data app, finding a Hollywood tabloid 'scandal' magazine, long since out of print in his own era, with an article about father and son. As Clay continued to enjoy the computer images, Terry read up on the famous model and his star son. Gay, married to an ex LAPD cop, associated with a top talent agent and a gay advocate lawyer. "His son is getting married? I thought Mark said it wasn't legal here."

"Huh? Not here. No. I think Alexander and Billy are tying the knot in New York."

Terry looked up the two names together, 'Alex and Billy'. "So, still not legal nation-wide. What a farce."

"Tell me about it."

"Would you marry me if I wanted to?" Terry asked, seeing an article about a tough SWAT lieutenant, Billy Sharpe marrying a man twenty years his junior, Alexander Richfield.

Clay spun around and gaped at Terry. "Are you just saying that to tease me?"

"No?" Terry assumed if they lived together…

Clay leapt out of his chair and landed on Terry. "Yes! Yes! Armand, yes!"

"Why didn't I ask you before?" Terry set his handheld computer down and hugged Clay.

"Oh, baby, I asked you and you said it was too soon. But I love you, I love you so much."

"Too soon? How long have we been together?"

"Nearly a month!"

Terry choked and his cheeks blushed. Rich older man, with big house, asks young twink to live with him? *Hmm. Uh oh.*

"I'm the happiest boy toy in So-Cal!" Clay nuzzled Terry's neck and ground his hips on Terry's lap.

Terry stared at the photos he had taken of Mark Richfield that were on his computer screen, and wondered if he had just made a huge mistake.

TiMELESS

CHAPTER 10

Clay insisted they go out for dinner in West Hollywood.

Though Terry lived in this area all his life, he didn't recognize much. Over the next fifty-five years many new businesses had sprung up and homes were upgraded. Only the street names were familiar, but all hopes of using landmarks to guide him were lost over time.

His phone buzzed in his pocket as Clay sat beside him, also using his phone to text or play games, Terry didn't know which.

"There!" Clay pointed. "You drove right passed the street."

"Oh. Sorry. Where should I park?"

"Where you always park." Clay didn't look up.

"And that is?"

Clay gave him a strange look. "Are you overtired or just preoccupied?"

"Both."

"The pay lot near the library."

Terry had no clue.

As if he were growing slightly frustrated, Clay pointed. "Right at the light. You never try for street parking."

"Some things never change." Terry knew even in the year 2035, there were too many cars in LA. But at least the smog was gone with the end of fossil fuels and clean alternatives were the only method to run a car.

He pulled up to the entrance and took a ticket out of the slot, allowing the arm to raise up and give them access. He parked in the first available space and climbed out, waiting for Clay to do the same before he used the key fob to activate the door locks and alarm. With a click the remote secured the sleek car and they began walking out of the cement lot to the street. While they did, Terry removed his phone to check who had text him. Beside him Clay was content to tap his thumbs into the keypad on the phone, not paying attention.

A text from someone named 'Neil Blanchard' read, '*hope ur having fun with ur money grubbin twink. ya fucker.*'

Terry stopped short and reread it. It was certainly meant to enflame, and not written as a joke.

"What?" Clay asked, also stopping and turning around.

"I got a text from Neil." Terry waited to see what reaction Clay gave.

Clay instantly grew furious. "Block him! I swear, Armand, he will never get over you if you let him contact you!" Clay leaned closer. "What did he say?"

Terry pocketed the phone. "Never mind."

"You're making me jealous. You don't still love him do you?"

Uh oh. Terry suddenly got a bad feeling in his stomach that Clay was not who he was here to see. *And I asked the kid to marry me. Damn.*

"Armand?" Clay clasped his hand and seemed slightly insecure suddenly. "Do you still love Neil?"

"I don't know what I feel." And that was the truth. Other than confusion, Terry was at a loss.

Clay seemed to develop a chip on his shoulder but kept quiet. He was led to a restaurant with a group of people lingering both outside and inside the lobby. Clay moved boldly through the crowd and said to the host, "Armand Legrand, table for two."

TiMELESS

As if his name was known, or held some clout, Clay smirked slightly as the host looked up passed Clay and directly into his eyes. And indeed, it made a difference.

"Yes, of course, Mr Legrand, allow me to bring you to the bar where you can have a drink until we prepare your special table."

The host escorted them through a packed room with bad acoustics and loud background music, making quiet conversation impossible. The host leaned over to the bartender, gestured to Clay and him, and nodded, as if communicating their importance. The bartender's expression lit up with delight and he met Terry's gaze.

"So good to have you dine with us tonight, Mr Legrand. Your usual?"

"Sure." Terry hoped it was better than a potent rum and coke ala Tom West.

Clay claimed Armand, holding him around the waist and leaning against him affectionately. He asked Armand, "Can I tell him we're toasting our engagement?"

"Uh, how about not yet. Not until I get you a ring or something."

"Mm." Clay kissed Armand's neck.

Many eyes caught the display, but none hostile. Even in 2012, West Hollywood was a safe haven for gay men and women, and Terry was happy to say two decades later, so much had happened to improve gay/civil rights, he was glad he was born when he had been, and not during a time of confusion for the American population, half of which was stuck in the mud of prehistoric days.

With the aroma of charred grilled food and garlic in the air, a martini glass was handed to Terry. The pink color made him smile. He thanked the bartender and sipped it. "Mm! Lovely." Terry had no idea what it was, but it was a mixture of sweet, tangy, and delicious.

Another cocktail was given to Clay. He tapped Terry's drink and said, "To us."

"To us." Terry's attention was distracted by the host who signaled to him. He followed the man to a gorgeous outdoor patio, strung with lights and packed with diners.

They were shown to a table near the corner, so Terry took the seat which had a grand view of the entire deck. Clay sat beside him and they were handed menus.

After placing his drink on the table, Terry took the menu.

"Your server will be right with you."

"Thanks." Terry glanced at the selection, pleased with the quality.

Another buzz in his pocket made him glance at Clay. Clay had his drink in one hand, sipping it, and reading the menu as it lay flat on the table.

Trying to be discreet, Terry took out the phone and read another angry text from Neil. *'Fuck u for bringing him to OUR place!'*

Terry jerked his head up and looked around the area, inspecting every individual. At the opposite end of the patio was a man, glaring with so much venom and hatred, Terry's hair stood on end. A woman was seated with Neil, also giving Terry a sneer.

"Shit." Terry could see from where he was empty glasses around Neil, as if he was drowning his sorrows. "Clay…"

"Hmm? Did you decide?"

"I think Neil is here."

Clay jerked his head up and immediately spotted him. "Ignore him, Armand."

"Uh, can I just at least go and try and make peace with him? He's shooting daggers at me."

"Fuck him!" Clay gave Neil the finger and the gesture seemed to enrage Neil excessively.

"Stop it." Terry swiped at Clay's hand to make him drop it. "One minute. Please."

"Fine, whatever." Clay picked up his phone and began texting.

TiMELESS

Terry moved out his chair and walked across the crowded deck to a man who appeared about to kill him. But…through that scowl, Terry could see…Sky.

He approached the man and woman and immediately the woman said, "I have to go to the ladies room." She left, nearly pushing Terry aside as she made her way, but her anger was obvious.

Neil sneered. "What the fuck do you want?"

"I'm sorry. I had no idea you'd be here."

"You fucking liar. We came here very Friday night. Fuck you!"

"Did you drive? Or did…" Terry gestured to the empty seat.

"Did? Olivia? Is that who you mean? Like you forgot her name as well as everything we ever meant to each other?"

Terry looked back at Clay and though he was pouting he was texting, ignoring him and Neil. Terry pointed to the empty chair beside Neil. "May I?"

"Fuck you!"

"I take that as a yes." Terry sat down and leaned closer to Neil, able to clearly see Sky in his eyes, even more than ever as they drew closer to the correct time frame he was aiming for in this crazy experiment. "Why did we break up?"

"You tell me? You asshole!"

"No. This time you tell me."

Neil became emotional and rubbed his face in anguish. "Armand, I'll give up the booze. I promise."

"Ah." Terry nodded. He looked down at the empty glasses. "How many have you had?"

"I swear. From now on. Take me back. Please. I know I fucked up."

"Do you go to AA?"

"I will. I swear." Neil reached out to touch Terry and the familiarity killed him. Sky's touch.

109

"We were together for six years, Armand." Neil began to cry. "You threw it away on that...kid? That wanna-be model who will leave you the minute he gets a paying gig?"

Terry glanced back at Clay, seeing his impatience, and with good reason. *First I ask the kid to marry me, then I hang out with my ex? No good.*

"So," Terry addressed Neil again, "It was the booze? That was it?"

Neil tilted his head in confusion. "That's what you told me. Why don't you tell me what else it was? I was happy." His expression changed drastically and tears ran down his cheeks. "I was so happy with you."

"Oh God." Terry reached out and held Neil, smelling Sky's scent on him and wanting to rub his body all over him.

"Uh hum!"

Terry parted from the embrace and wiped his eyes and nose as he too grew upset. Clay was standing there, hands on hips. "Well? What the fuck, Armand?"

"Clay. I'm sorry." Terry began to sob, hearing Neil crying beside him. "I'm not over Sky...uh, Neil."

Clay gave him a nasty glare. "I am so over you!" He flipped Terry off and left the patio.

Neil's lip quivered and his eyes ran with tears. "Baby."

Terry embraced him and rocked him, holding him so tight he wanted to die in his arms.

"Finally!" Olivia said, picking up her purse. "You boys have make up sex and forgive each other, okay? I'll call you, Neil."

"See ya. Thanks, Olivia." Neil used the napkin to wipe his eyes.

"Let me pay for the drinks I had and I'll drive you home." Terry took his wallet out of his pocket.

"I can drive. I'm okay."

TiMELESS

Immediately Terry reacted. "No fucking way, Neil. This is what I am talking about. Drinking and driving."

"I had two. And dinner. I'm fine."

Two meant four, at least. Terry leaned on the table and made sure Neil looked into his eyes. "I will not allow you to drive. You want me back? You have to live with my fucking rules about you, driving and booze."

"Yes." Neil nodded. "I'm sorry. Yes."

"We'll get your car tomorrow." Terry stood and returned to his table, tossing cash on it. The waiter appeared, looking confused.

"Is that enough to cover the drinks?" Terry asked.

"Yes. Was there something wrong?"

"Not with the service. Just have to go."

"I'm sorry, sir."

"No need." Terry patted his arm and returned to see Neil, staggering to his feet, obviously far from sober. Terry approached him as Neil took his credit card from his wallet and gave it to a waiter to pay the tab.

"Sit down before you fall on your face." Terry nudged Neil back to his chair.

"I'm sorry. Armand, I was so upset when you broke up with me..."

"That you drank? That you did exactly what broke us up?"

"Forgive me." Neil's eyes overflowed.

Terry's heart was in agony. "Always. I forgive you. I didn't that night...oh God. You left so angry, and I never got my chance."

"You had a million chances. I begged to meet with you. Texted you to see me."

"No. Not that." Terry rubbed his face and tried not to make too much of a scene. Two men crying on the patio of a pricy WeHo restaurant was enough. Last thing he wanted to do was wail like he did...like he did...at Sky's grave.

111

"Take me home." Neil's eyes were overflowing.

The waiter brought the credit slip and Terry watched Neil sign it, feeling so sick to his stomach he could not think straight. Was this it? Was this the chance to change history?

Terry held Neil close as they walked outside, headed back to the parking garage. He felt Neil lean against him and the familiarity was too much for Terry. He started to cry again.

Neil held him tighter, and they walked to the multi-story building as Terry struggled to remember where he parked. "Christ, where is the damn car?"

"You always did forget. Too much on your mind." Neil smiled.

"Yes. It's true. My work. It's always been my heaven and my hell."

"I know." Neil hugged him with one arm around Terry's waist as they figured out where Terry had parked. Once they were seated in Terry's car, he turned his knees to face Neil, caressing his soft hair and staring into familiar eyes.

"Has Clay got a lot of things at the house?"

"I don't know."

Neil nodded, not adding to that topic. "A man can change, Terry."

"I..." Terry looked up. "Did. Did you call me 'Terry'?"

Neil stared into his eyes, deeply, so intensely Terry felt as if Sky was with him, with him right here, right now.

"I don't know why I called you that. I'm sorry."

"No!" Terry cupped Neil's face. "Look at me!"

Neil did. The gaze made Terry's stomach pinch. "Sky?" he whispered.

"Sky..." Neil said, as if musing. "Why do I know that name?"

"Sky Norwood? You know that name?"

"I should. I should!"

"Do you know Terry Lennox too?"

TiMELESS

Neil rubbed his forehead as if it ached. "Who are they? Why do those names make my skin prickle with goose bumps?"

"Please don't freak out at what I am going to tell you." He held Neil's face in his hand, making him look into his gaze.

Neil nodded in the confining grip of Terry's hold.

After exhaling a low breath, Terry said, "We are always going to be together, you and I."

"I know. I love you...so much." Neil's eyes began to fill.

"I mean, spanning time. Timeless."

"Oh, God, Armand..." Neil began to break down.

"Do you believe in reincarnation? In life after life? In anything like that?"

"I don't disbelieve it."

"I..." Terry knew he tried to explain this before and failed, and 'leaped' out of that era to another. He looked up at the roof of the car and pleaded with an invisible force, "Let me stay."

"Huh? Stay? Where are you going, Armand?"

"Nowhere, I hope. Look, lover, you and I, we are destined to repeat this until we get it right."

"I'm sorry. I promise to go to AA."

"No. I'm talking bigger. Like...like," Terry bit his lip and said something that sounded stupid to him. "Soul mates? You believe in those?"

"You are mine. I have always wanted you, from the first minute I spotted you at that New Year's Eve party six years ago."

Terry began to smile. "Yes. I remember that."

"We kissed at midnight."

"We did." Terry laughed and combed his fingers back through Neil's hair.

"Is that what you mean?"

"Sure. Yes." What was Terry supposed to say? He was a man from 2055? On a mission to stop the death of his lover but getting

113

stuck in strange bodies and eras that didn't make sense to him? It was absurd.

Neil cupped the back of Terry's head and brought him to his lips. When they touched, Terry was so elated at the kiss of his lover, one he missed so much, hot tears ran from his eyes.

"Take me home. Make love to me." Neil wiped the tears from Terry's cheeks.

"God. I'm terrified to start this car."

"Why? What will happen?"

"We'll get hit head on. You'll die. I'll survive, barely."

"Why do you think that's going to occur?" Neil took Terry's hand into his.

"Because it has, before. At first you just got yourself killed, then..." Terry shut up, seeing the fear in Neil's eyes.

"No." Neil shook his head. "Nothing's going to happen."

"It will. Inevitably. I am finding out I can't change fate, and it's driving me out of my mind." Terry coughed on his sob and ran his hand over his hair.

"Fate gave you to me." Neil kissed Terry's knuckles. "That fact it can't take away."

"But it keeps taking you away from me!" Terry sat facing forward and stared at the parked cars in the cement lot.

"But we always manage to find each other. Right? You said we're soul mates? Reincarnation?"

"I don't want to keep losing you. The pain is too much. I'm trying to break the pattern. I can't. I can't." Terry clenched his fists.

"Do you believe love conquers all?"

"Yes, in some ways. I mean, it triumphs over hate. But over death? I'm not so sure." He wiped his eyes.

"When you lose someone you love, they are always in your heart."

TiMELESS

"Yes!" Terry grew angry. "But they are gone from my life! My house! My bed!" He sobbed and sank into the bucket seat. "I can't drive anywhere. I will lose everything. I can't."

"So we're going to sit here? For? How long?"

"We'll walk. We'll take a cab." Terry touched the door handle.

"If fate means to take me, do you really think you can change it by altering our mode of transportation?"

"You die in a car!" Terry yelled and then quieted his voice. "I'll walk to Bel Air if I have to. I can't see this happen again. I'm worn out. I'm exhausted and empty."

"Even if we did, a car would probably drive on the sidewalk and the result would be the same."

"Sky," Terry reached for him. "No. Don't say that. Sometimes we can change fate if we try."

"Maybe the lesson, Terry, is to enjoy what you have while you have it. And not squander the moments."

"No one can live like that. Work is consuming, *life* is consuming. Even though I love you, love you like no one ever before, it's impossible to not take things for granted, to not expect you to be...be in my bed every night, in my arms... did you call me Terry again?"

"Yes. Terry. I know you have tried to find a way. A way back to that night."

"Sky. Please. If you know, fight with me."

"How? You are the one with the technology. I live here. Now." He gestured to the surroundings. "2012. This is my reality. I am a man in love with a photographer named Armand Legrand. This is who I am."

"And..." Terry could barely hold it together. "It ends tonight? Again? All we worked for? You so young?"

"Fate. I can't control it, and I doubt you can either, Terry. You are just going to suffer my death again and again."

"Fuck!" Terry hit the steering wheel with heel of his palm.

Sky reached to hold Terry, pulling him close over the console and kissing his hair tenderly.

"No. I won't give up! There has to be a way of changing fate. Has to."

"Babe. We have each other now. You came back to me tonight. I didn't die without you."

Terry covered his face, pulled out of Sky's arms and curled into a ball in agony. Sky caressed his hair gently in comfort.

Terry refused to turn the engine on or drive an inch. There had to be a magic hour, and he was going to wait it out. He'd go to hell and back if he had to. He'd already been there.

TiMELESS

CHAPTER 11

...there's nothing we can do. We've lost contact with him now. I have no idea how to bring him back.

Was he successful?

I can check the data base on the obit-macularly standard to see the dates of descention...wait...there seems to be something happening. Look at the transcoded biopulary kilgard data. It states a man named...Neil Blanchard died...hang on...no. This can't be right.

What is it, doctor?

Did he do it? Did Dr Lennox alter fate? No!

But how can we know if we can't communicate with him or bring him back? We have nothing to certify the event took place back in 2012.

This obit-file contains every death of every individual in the United States for the last century. Neil Blanchard did not die at age thirty-one. He died nearly fifty years later.

What about the other man? Armand?

Died at age eighty, same month, same day as Neil.

Suicide pact?

Nothing listed on the data. Look, what do we do? We can't get him back and if we did, he'd suffer the same thing he wanted to prevent, creating this experiment. Wait a minute!

What, Doctor?

I have no birth record of Sky Norwood or...Terry Lennox in 2035!

What does that mean?

My word. He did it. He changed history.

But we have no contact with him! We can't get him back!

No. We can't. And maybe he doesn't need to come back. Maybe he's where he should be.

He will be sorely missed.

Not nearly as much as he would be if we brought him back now.

I agree, Doctor. There's nothing we can do.

Armand woke with a start and looked around. He was sleeping in the front seat of his sports car in a parking garage. He rubbed his face and looked beside him. Neil was leaning against the door, also sound asleep.

"Wow. How drunk did we get?" Armand checked his watch. It was nine in the morning. "Babe?"

"Hmm?" Neil was slow to stir.

"We fell asleep in the car. You believe this?" Armand started the engine and looked at the ticket to see when he had parked the night before. "This is going to cost us a mint."

Neil sat upright and rubbed his face. "How the hell did we fall asleep here?" He took out his wallet and removed a twenty.

"Hell if I know. But I need to get us home."

"You okay to drive?"

"Yeah." Armand drove slowly around the narrow opening between parked vehicles to the exit gate. He handed the attendant his ticket and the man glanced at him for a moment before he said, "Eighteen dollars, please."

"Ouch." Armand handed the man the twenty and was given change. He gave it to Neil and pulled out to the stop sign before heading home. "I feel like I've been in a coma."

TiMELESS

"I know. Right?"

Armand headed to the house he and Neil shared in Bel Air. "At least we got over our differences. I'm sorry, Neil. I should never have been so hard on you."

"No. You have every right. I fucked up." He held Armand's hand and kissed it.

Armand clasped Neil's hand tightly as he drove, seeing very light traffic on this Saturday morning. He pulled into his driveway and elevated the garage.

"You think Clay packed his stuff?" Neil exited the car and walked to the door connecting the kitchen to the garage. He paused. "The house is not armed."

"Then, yes. He did." Armand shook his head sadly and said, "I'm sorry, Neil. It was impulsive to ask him to move in. I swear he stayed over one night and ended up sinking in roots and living with me."

"Believe me. I know Clay and what he's like." Neil walked through the house to the bedroom. "Yes. He's been here."

Armand followed Neil to the bedroom and could see drawers opened and the framed picture of Clay had been removed.

"You think he stole anything?" Neil peered into the closet.

"No. He's not like that." Armand had a thought and checked his digital camera from the shoot he had the day before with Mark Richfield. It was in its case. He exhaled with relief.

"I need a shower. I feel like I slept in a car," Neil said, laughing.

"Babe." Armand reached for him and Neil fell into his embrace. "Let's never break up like that again."

"I know. It was a mistake. I'm so sorry, Armand."

Armand hugged him, loving the connections of their two bodies. A sensation of something very strong passed over him, so powerful he felt his body tingle and his toes go numb. He hung onto Neil waiting for it to pass since it was making him slightly dizzy.

119

"Wow." Armand held tighter. "I think I should eat something. I'm lightheaded."

"I got you. I got you and I won't ever let you go."

With his eyes closed, Armand saw a vision of men in lab coats. He tried to shake his head to rid it, it was so bizarre. One man turned to him in the vision and said, "*Congratulations, Dr Lennox. Your experiment was a success. Enjoy your life with Sky, but we shall miss you.*"

Armand shivered and closed his eyes tighter.

"Let's clean up, babe." Neil rubbed Armand's back gently.

Armand opened his eyes and stared at Neil, his lush brown irises and dark eyelashes. In Neil's eyes Armand could see he had everything he had ever hoped for; his future and his past.

"Yes. Let's shower. I need my man naked and wet."

Neil laughed seductively and they began stripping off their clothing. Their garments in a pile at their feet, Armand led the way to the bathroom, reaching into the shower stall to turn on the water. When he did, Neil asked, "When did you get that?"

"Get what?" Armand tried to see what he meant.

"That tat."

Using the bathroom vanity mirror, Armand peered into it to see a black tattoo on his low back. "What does it say?"

"You're asking me?" Neil laughed.

"Please don't tell me it says Clay Burrows."

"No, thank fuck. It says, '*love is timeless*'. I like it."

For the life of him Armand couldn't recall getting it done. He stepped into the shower and struggled with a sense of disorientation. As he soaked under the hot spray, Neil climbed in behind him, holding him and kissing him.

Armand spun around to face him. "I feel like we spent more time than one night sleeping in that car."

TIMELESS

"I hope we never do that again. I am sworn off booze, for- ever!" Neil held up his hand in an oath.

"Yeah. Me too. That was one of the weirdest nights I've had in a very long time."

"I can't remember much. Just you coming into the restaurant patio with Clay-the-leech."

"I'm sorry. Neil, forgive me." Armand pushed his crotch against Neil's and felt the water running between their bodies.

"Don't say you're sorry. Your love is the reason I'm here."

Another strange wave of dizziness sought to overwhelm Armand. He held onto Neil and closed his eyes again.

"I've got you. I'll never let you go." Neil rocked him, kissing his neck.

Armand had a feeling destiny had made her move, and though he wasn't a believer in fate, he had a sense it believed in him.

"I love you, Neil."

"You too, my lover. Love is timeless…truly."

Armand gazed into Neil's eyes and smiled.

~

Terry…can you hear me? It's Sky. Look, I know all you went through for me. I can't thank you enough. Never forget our love. Never forget what each day means and how quickly it can change. Hold onto your man and forgive him. But never let him go. I love you, Terry. I love you.

~

121

He opened his eyes and sat up.

It was dark in the room and he'd just had one of the most bizarre dreams he could recall. He looked around the bedroom and noticed he was not alone. He touched the warm body beside him.

The man opened his eyes and smiled. "What's up, babe?"

"Nothing. Go back to sleep. I just had a weird dream, that's all."

He was brought closer with an outstretched arm, overlapping bodies under the blanket. Letting out a deep sigh, he held tight and closed his eyes.

"I got ya. I'm not going anywhere."

Armand nuzzled against Neil, and felt sure, he and Neil had many years to be together, and share their lives.

THE END

About the Author

Award-winning author G.A. Hauser was born in Fair Lawn, New Jersey, USA and attended university in New York City. She moved to Seattle, Washington where she worked as a patrol officer with the Seattle Police Department. In early 2000 G.A. moved to Hertfordshire, England where she began her writing in earnest and published her first book, In the Shadow of Alexander. Now a full-time writer, G.A. has written over eighty novels, including several best-sellers of gay fiction. GA is also the Executive Producer for her first feature film, CAPITAL GAMES. For more information on other books by G.A., visit the author at her official website. www.authorgahauser.com

G.A. has won awards from All Romance eBooks for Best Author 2010, 2009, Best Novel 2008, *Mile High*, and Best Author 2008, Best Novel 2007, *Secrets and Misdemeanors*, Best Author 2007.

The G.A. Hauser Collection

Single Titles

Unnecessary Roughness

Hot Rod

Mr. Right

Happy Endings

Down and Dirty

Lancelot in Love

Cowboy Blues

Midnight in London

Living Dangerously

The Last Hard Man

Taking Ryan

Born to be Wilde

The Adonis of WeHo

Boys

Band of Brothers

Rough Ride

I Love You I Hate You

Code Red

Timeless

TiMELESS

Marry Me
The Farmer's Son
One Two Three
L.A. Masquerade
Dude! Did You Just Bite Me?
My Best Friend's Boyfriend
The Diamond Stud
The Hard Way
Games Men Play
Born to Please
Of Wolves and Men
The Order of Wolves
Got Men?
Heart of Steele
All Man
Julian
Black Leather Phoenix
London, Bloody, London
In The Dark and What Should Never Be, Erotic Short
Stories
Mark and Sharon
A Man's Best Friend

125

G. A. HAUSER

It Takes a Man

Blind Ambition (formerly The Physician and the Actor)

For Love and Money

The Kiss

Naked Dragon

Secrets and Misdemeanors

Capital Games

Giving Up the Ghost

To Have and To Hostage

Love you, Loveday

The Boy Next Door

When Adam Met Jack

Exposure

The Vampire and the Man-eater

Murphy's Hero

Mark Antonious deMontford

Prince of Servitude

Calling Dr Love

The Rape of St. Peter

The Wedding Planner

Going Deep

Double Trouble

TiMELESS

Pirates

Miller's Tale

Vampire Nights

Teacher's Pet

In the Shadow of Alexander

The Rise and Fall of the Sacred Band of Thebes

The Action Series

Acting Naughty

Playing Dirty

Getting it in the End

Behaving Badly

Dripping Hot

Packing Heat

Being Screwed

Something Sexy

Going Wild

Having it All!

Bending the Rules

Keeping it Up

Men in Motion Series

Mile High

Cruising

Driving Hard

Leather Boys

Heroes Series

Man to Man

Two In Two Out

Top Men

G.A. Hauser

Writing as Amanda Winters

Sister Moonshine

Nothing Like Romance

Silent Reign

Butterfly Suicide

Mutley's Crew

TiMELESS

At Your Service, Staff Sergeant Gary Wilson

(Short bite based on the characters of ALL MAN)

Gary knew damn well what showing up in his Airman's Battle Uniform did to Chase. It drove Chase wild.

It was impossible to have Chase working at the clinic at Wright Patterson Air Base and not seek him out. And Gary knew he was being naughty, but hell, after three tours, two in Iraq and one in Afghanistan, he deserved a little, 'naughty'.

Entering the clinic, Gary removed his cap and approached the reception desk. "Hello, I'm Staff Sgt. Wilson. I need to see Chase Arlington, please."

"I think he's with a patient." The woman smiled dreamily at him. "I can check."

"I don't want to interrupt him. It's not urgent." *Like hell it ain't.*

"I can check, Sergeant. Can you have a seat?"

Gary had a quick look at the waiting area and the few civilian patients staring at him. "That's fine. Could you just say someone from the 445th is here? He doesn't need my name." Gary knew that would ruin the surprise.

"I'll let him know."

"Thank you, ma'am." Gary nodded politely.

129

When she passed into physical therapy area, Gary ducked out of view. A moment later she returned. "He's just finishing up, Sergeant."

"Thank you, ma'am."

"You're very welcome." She returned to her desk, smiling flirtatiously at him.

Gary checked his watch. He didn't have a lot of time either.

Finally an older man left the therapy room. A moment later, Chase appeared looking around the waiting area.

Moving from behind the potted fichus tree, Gary met Chase's dark eyes. The moment of recognition and fire that passed over Chase's face was priceless.

He leaned over the desk to the same receptionist. "I'm taking a quick break. Be right back."

"Fine, Mr. Arlington."

Gary exited the clinic, popping his cap back on his head. He was grinning so hard his cheeks ached. Feeling Chase's hand on his arm, Gary grew even more thrilled. He knew what Chase's reaction would be. Did he know him, or did he know him?

Chase directed Gary through the parking lot, behind the clinic near some tall barren oak trees waving in the cool breeze.

"Get over here!" Chase hissed in desperation.

TiMELESS

Gary was urged back against the brick wall of the building with Chase's hot body pressed against his. At the taste of Chase's lips, Gary closed his eyes and held his waist tightly.

As predicted, Chase went mad. He ran his hands all over Gary's uniform, from his shoulders, down his chest, his crotch, back up to his arms, then Chase took the ride all over again, the entire time whimpering in agony.

Gary parted from his lips to grin wickedly at him. "Knew you'd go nuts."

"I love you in this thing! Ah!" Chase took a quick glance around before he opened Gary's zipper.

"Geez! I thought I'd be sucking you off!" Gary pressed against the cold brick wall behind him. "Mother-fucker!" Instantly Chase was kneeling in front of him sucking him fast and hard.

Gary's head started spinning from the daring deed. They both knew if they were caught doing this on base there would be dire consequences. That slightly amused Gary. After what he'd been through in the war, he didn't think what he was doing was all that dangerous.

When Chase's fingers dug under Gary's balls, Gary lit up. "Ahhfuck! Chase, I'm there!"

Chase drew harder, deeper.

Gary closed his eyes and shuddered as he came in Chase's mouth. "Holy shit."

Taking his time milking Gary's cock, Chase finally stood, tucking Gary back into his camouflaged trousers.

The minute he had, Gary spun them around, slamming Chase against the wall. He dropped to his knees to return the favor. Feeling his hat being removed as he exposed Chase's dick, Gary glanced up at Chase just before he slid Chase's cock into his mouth. Chase had popped Gary's cap on his own head. Trying not to laugh while a big hard dick was between his lips, Gary focused on the job at hand, knowing damn well time was of the essence.

The taste and scent of Chase's body was worth the risk. It was worth everything to Gary.

"Look at you..." Chase crooned, running his hands through Gary's dark short hair. "You gorgeous soldier, I am so fucking in love with you."

Gary intensified the sucking. If Chase could talk, he wasn't swooning enough by his standards. He yanked Chase's trousers wider to get at his balls and ass. It did the trick.

Chase's body tensed up and his cock went rock hard. "Oh, Christ..."

TiMELESS

Gary closed his eyes as Chase climaxed, feeling his come shoot into his mouth in ecstasy. Sucking him until nothing more came out, Gary pulled up Chase's zipper, buttoned his fly and caught his breath.

Chase, still wearing Gary's ABU hat, was recuperating slowly.

"You look damn cute in that thing," Gary laughed, pecking Chase's lips.

"Not as beautiful as you, soldier." Chase handed it back to him.

"I have to go." Gary took one last minute to crush Chase against the brick wall and kiss him. "Until later."

"Yes. Tonight." Chase looked positively dazed.

Gary flipped his cap back on his head and gave Chase a proper military salute. "Permission to leave, sir!" Gary teased.

"Regretfully, permission granted." Chase walked back around to the parking lot with him. "Just remember something, Staff Sergeant Wilson."

"Yes?" Gary grinned wickedly at him.

"Chase Arlington, lowly civilian, is at your service. Night and day."

"I like that," Gary purred. "Later, civie." Gary waved as he jogged across the lot back to his Hummer. Seeing Chase still standing in the cool October breeze watching him, Gary waved.

Once he was headed back to his area on the base, he checked the rear view mirror quickly. A drop of Chase's come was on his cheek. He wiped it off and with a wicked smile, sucked at his finger.

~

Chase waited until he couldn't see the Hummer any longer. Making his way back inside the clinic, Chase smiled. *At your service, Sgt. Wilson. On call.*

"Everything all right, Mr. Arlington?"

Chase addressed the receptionist, "Yes, everything is fine. It's my pleasure to serve the men who serve our country," Chase boasted.

"I couldn't agree more." She smiled.

Dying for the rest of the afternoon to pass so he could have Gary in his arms again, Chase returned to his work, floating on a cloud.

TiMELESS

For Sam

(Short bite based on the characters of **Leather Boys**)

Devlin burrowed his face between Sam's thighs. There was nothing as sweet as sucking on a man he loved like no other before him. Mouthing Sam's balls, rubbing his face all over his body, hearing him moan. It was worth everything Dev owned.

Their playtime. Fantasies to make their hearts pound, their mouths water. *Whose turn is it tonight?* Dev loved that question. He won either way. And tonight, it was his. Sam. Big beautiful Sam tied up. Did it get any better than that?

Dev doubted it.

And there was no doubt Sam was in heaven. Just the moans and gasping were enough to let Dev know he was floating.

Pausing, having to look up at him again just to admire him, Dev caught his breath as he stared, and stared. Sam's chest heaved with his excitement. His wrists and ankles tied to the bedposts, naked, vulnerable, and delicious. Sliding off the foot of the bed, Dev rubbed his hands down the leather jeans he was wearing. He was hot and dying to take them off, but that wasn't the fantasy.

Sam opened his blue eyes with a look of longing Dev knew he would remember forever.

Wanting his mouth, Dev crawled up Sam's body, slowly, a wicked smile on his lips.

"Ah!" Sam gasped.

"What?" Dev paused.

"Leather! Stick!"

Dev peered down. The leather of his jeans had stuck to Sam's hot dick. Backing up, Dev decided the kiss could wait. He enveloped Sam's cock instead, sucking to the base, whimpering in ecstasy. After Sam had writhed on the bed in anticipation, Dev allowed Sam's cock to slip back out of his mouth. When he had the attention of those brilliant sky blue eyes, Dev whispered, "I love you, Sam. I always will."

Sam's response was a mixture of his lust and his adoration. "I know, babe. I feel the same."

"For Sam..." Dev grabbed the base of Sam's cock. This time he would make him come.

"For me. Ah!" Sam hissed, arching his back from the intensity of the approaching climax.

TIMELESS

Once Dev had tasted Sam's come in delight, he sat back and eyed him one last time. He knew, if he lost this man, he would never find a replacement. And he was right.

21461522R00073

Made in the USA
Lexington, KY
16 March 2013